# SCENTS AND A SUSPECT

ACCIDENTAL GHOST DETECTIVE AGENCY SERIES
BOOK 1

EMMIE LYN

Copyright © 2022 by Emmie Lyn

All rights reserved. Except as permitted under the U.S. Copyright Act of 1976, no part of this publication may be reproduced, distributed or transmitted in any form or by any means, or stored in a database or retrieval system without the prior written permission of the publisher.

Editor: Helen Page

Proofreader: Sara Miller

Cover Designer: Mayflower Studio

This is a work of fiction. Names, characters, organizations, places, events, and incidents are either products of the author's imagination or are used fictitiously. Any resemblance to actual persons, living or dead, or actual events is purely coincidental. No part of this work may be reproduced, or stored in a retrieval system, or transmitted in any form or by any means, electronic, mechanical, photocopying, recording, or otherwise, without written permission of the publisher.

Whiskered Mysteries<br>https://whiskeredmysteries.com

*For all my readers...thank you! I love sharing my twisty cozy mysteries with you.*

[Click here to sign up for my newsletter and never miss a new release.](#)

# ABOUT THIS BOOK

When Nikki Knight returns to her childhood stomping grounds in Frog Hollow Georgia, she realizes life has become nuttier than the pecan muffins at her late grandmother's haunted B&B. But the only ghost in the Moonlight Mansion is the previous lady of the house, still roaming the halls in her afterlife.

Not ten steps into town, Nikki finds herself with a furry new companion. An abandoned royal dachshund who just might carry the secret to his past owner's untimely demise. But when Nikki is seen snooping around at one too many crime scenes, the local officer becomes suspicious and begins popping up where she least expects him.

Now, she needs to find out what happened ASAP and protect Prince Dasher Dangerdog Bean from falling into the wrong—and deadly—hands.

Can Nikki and her royal dachshund solve the case? Or will they end up roaming the Moonlight Mansion with her grandmother?

# 1

When I hit the Frog Hollow town line in Peach Plains, Georgia, my rental car rolled into the gas station on the fumes left in the tank. I filled up and slid back onto the soft seat, impatient to get to Moonlight Mansion. But when I turned the key, one small problem stood in my way.

Actually, the problem sat ten feet in front of my car, staring at me like he expected something. Maybe a ride?

I walked over to the dog, crouched in front of him, and extended my hand. "Are you lost?" I asked.

Of course, he didn't answer, but he gave my fingers a lick, then he trotted to my open door with all the confidence in the world and jumped in.

No one else was around to claim the dog this early. Me, being me, there was no way I'd leave this poor guy stranded. So, I did what any dog lover would do. I followed him to my car. "You can come with me," I said, my habit of talking to animals reinforced after my solitary drive from Blueberry Bay in coastal Maine.

At this point, I think I'd talk to a turnip. But instead, I

turned to the adorable dachshund and said, "We'll sort out where you belong later. But you have to sit in the back. Understand?"

He jumped to the center of the back seat like he owned the place. And curiously, like he understood me.

I laughed and shook my head. The miles had gotten to me. The dog was just well-trained I told myself.

I buckled myself in again and continued on the last fifteen minutes of my journey. I cast an eye now and then to my rearview mirror to check on my passenger. He seemed perfectly content watching the world pass by through the window.

When I arrived at the entrance to Moonlight Mansion, I stopped, rolled down the window of my rented red BMW convertible, and inhaled the pungent aroma of... a wet towel rolled around a bouquet of lilac blossoms. The scent wafted around me and triggered memories like a gong clanging in my head.

This smell—swampy and slightly sweet at the same time—welcomed me back to Frog Hollow, a medium-sized, mostly quiet town in the Peach Plains region of Georgia.

When the wind blew in the right direction, the swampy, decaying whiff caused some noses to wrinkle and even get pinched. It wasn't awful to me, just a part of Frog Hollow's big picture. I was used to it. I mean, with a name like Frog Hollow, what did anyone expect? Maybe dry desert air? Not a chance. Not here in Georgia. After all, I'd spent many of my thirty-two summers sniffing the air here at Moonlight Mansion.

Mist swirled around my car on this muggy May morning. I swatted away a few mosquitoes buzzing around the messy bun I'd piled on my head like they were deciding where to land. Now that I was here, my emotions bubbled to the surface, jumping between pleasant and horrible.

On the one hand, I had boatloads of wonderful childhood memories. Catching frogs, lots and lots of frogs, learning to ride my first bike with purple tassels on the handlebars, and sitting next to my grandmother's koi pond eating peach ice cream, most of it dripping down my chin. Those memories and more came to mind bringing a smile to my lips.

You get the picture, right? I enjoyed such a lazy, fun childhood, you'd be forgiven for thinking I was spoiled. But trust me, Audrey did not allow that.

So why did a pall hang over me as the mansion came into view?

My most recent memory came back like someone had thrust a dagger into my gut. I guess that best describes what happened a few short months ago when my grandmother, Audrey, was murdered.

I sighed, wishing I could change the past. But life doesn't work that way. That single event turned my world upside down and inside out.

For lack of any other way to deal with this sudden stab of sadness, I channeled Audrey—my rock, my motivation, and most of all, the one who loved me unconditionally. Just thinking about her conjured up a vision of her so real it brought me back to the day she had made a promise: *Nikki? Don't forget, one day, this will all be yours, so keep your head up, keep your smile bright and shiny, and never, ever let anyone know what you're really thinking.*

I planned to honor her memory and live by that advice no matter what lay ahead. Since Audrey liked to cover her bases and get what she wanted—even after death—here I was, taking over her pride and joy.

Was I up to this new challenge? I hoped so. If necessary, I'd dig to the middle of the earth to succeed in this new adventure.

First though, before I drove up the driveway, I climbed out of my rental car. Next to me was the stone pillar that marked the entrance to my new legacy—the rambling Moonlight Mansion Bed and Breakfast, ten acres of lawns, gardens, and trees draped with Spanish moss.

While I pondered everything that Moonlight Mansion meant to me, Freda, the stone frog, stared down from her perch on the top of the pillar that marked the driveway entrance. She quietly surveyed the comings and goings of the mansion. She'd taught me that silence could be a powerful weapon, a lesson I struggled to remember when my emotions threatened to erupt like an overflowing volcano.

The crunch of tires on Live Oak Lane interrupted my musings and the mosquito symphony buzzing around my face. The approaching car slowed and stopped next to me.

A bleached blonde with purple highlights popped her head out the window and shouted, "Is that you, Nikki Knight? I heard you were coming back to town. I'll have to sound the alarm and let everyone know you really are here."

I hadn't seen Lacey May Dawson for a year or two, but we'd beaten the same paths as teenagers for many summers when I was here visiting my grandmother. She laughed as her dark eyes seemed to caress my sweet ride. Based on the rust bucket she drove and how she tightened her fingers around the steering wheel, her laugh didn't fool me for one nanosecond. She was jealous. Lacey May had always judged people—and when I say people, I meant the boys in town—by the car they owned. She liked them fast and flashy—the boys and the cars.

"Yes, Lacey May—"

"Just Lacey," she said sternly. Then she corrected me. "Lacey May was my mom. I dropped the May after she died and left me with a pile of debt. It's just Lacey now."

I'd heard that she'd changed her name, but I liked to remind her that I knew her back when she was Lacey May—the teenager with loose lips and sticky fingers. I wondered if much had changed besides her name and her hairdo, the size of a big old wasp nest.

"In case you hadn't heard, I have my own beauty salon now, Shear Magic. Swing by sometime, and I'll give those locks of yours a taming. Or," she winked, "I also do house calls. See you around, darlin'."

She hit the gas and sent gravel flying as she sped away. Either she was late for an important date, or she couldn't get away from me fast enough. Probably the latter, since an element of competition had always strained our friendship.

"What do you think, Freda?" I asked my silent friend.

But, like always, Freda kept her opinions to herself.

I let out another long sigh, patting the messy bun to check if I needed a touch-up. Obviously, Lacey's comment got to me. My thick wavy light brown curls always misbehaved, but no more than usual. I doubted Lacey had special talents that could help.

It was time to move forward and put memories of Lacey in the back of my mind. No more procrastinating.

I slid back onto the buttery soft seat of the BMW. This flashy rental was more than a mere splurge or a device just to show up Lacey. When I put it through its paces, I was looking for a match for my personality. I needed a sleek, responsive, and in-your-face new acquisition to announce my return to Frog Hollow. Nothing less than a statement car that said here-I-am-and-watch-out would do.

Audrey always stressed that I should be the baddest girl around. By baddest, she meant strong. I tried to live up to her expectations, but most of the time, I fell short. I hoped the candy-apple red BMW would let people know I was back with a splash. That a first impression of arriving in a glitzy car would put everyone on notice that I, Nikki Knight, was no shrinking violet. After all, this impression was important. No crawling back to Frog Hollow in the dead of night for me after my grandmother's scandalous murder. I was back, and I planned to be ready for whatever came my way.

Some folks would certainly roll their eyes dismissively and see me as too inexperienced to run Moonlight Mansion. But I'd simply prove the skeptics wrong. I couldn't care less what the so-called good people of Frog Hollow thought about me.

Since this town wasn't the typical touristy, activity-fueled venue, being tough would be a piece of cake. Tough and smart? No problem. Add a big dollop of peach ice cream to that cake, and I was in business. Without breaking a sweat.

I pulled my door closed like it signaled the end of the old carefree and fancy-free Nikki Knight. Hello to responsibility, the future, and new adventures. I was raring to go.

I glanced in the rearview mirror.

My back-seat passenger thumped his tail on the rich white leather.

"We're almost there. Once I'm settled, I'll try to figure out where you came from and get you back where you belong. How does that sound?" I said to the short-legged, long-bodied, black and brown fur-covered dachshund.

Of course he didn't answer, but he looked at me with intelligent, confident eyes. He had to belong to someone, and I suspected he was missing that someone. I sure wished he could tell me his story.

I presumed that finding his person would be the easiest task to check off my I'm-back list.

The Beemer tires crunched on the gravel as I followed the winding drive to the main house. I parked in the spot reserved for the owner of Moonlight Mansion—yours truly. I still had trouble wrapping my head around all this new responsibility. Was I up to it, I wondered again? I had no choice seeing as Audrey's will stipulated that I had to live here. I couldn't sell it.

My biggest concern was what lay ahead. Would I die of boredom? Audrey had always provided loads of excitement during my past visits, but well... a tear slid down my cheek as I wondered how I'd manage without her.

I *could* run this place. If Audrey had that much confidence in my abilities, I'd prove her right and then some.

With that tiny moment of worry out of the way, I turned off the ignition.

My heart raced as I thought of the best part of my new life, Miss Birdie Bell Long, waiting for me only a mere hundred yards away.

Birdie ran the place. She was a part of Moonlight Mansion, like the antique Victorian furniture and handmade quilts that gave the mansion its unique character. Without Birdie, Moonlight Mansion would be just another run-of-the-mill bed and breakfast with a bland personality.

She brought stability, order, and her dry, sassy style that wasn't always appreciated by some, but don't put me in that group. Plus, just thinking about her amazing blue-ribbon fried chicken made me drool. Second to none in this part of the world, her recipe remained a secret that she held close to her heart.

I loved Birdie like a sister, or maybe a doting aunt who spoiled me but at the same time never hesitated to show me her upturned eyebrow when necessary. That was more than enough to remind me to watch my step.

Not more than a second later, the front door of the mansion swung wide open. Light poured out from behind the big heavy double door. Centered in the light stood Birdie, dressed in a riot of color. Her red hair, needing more than a simple comb, was the exact sight I craved. She flung her arms flung wide in the welcome I needed, exuding familiarity, love, and the expectation of a big breakfast.

I jumped out of the Beemer and opened the door for my back-seat passenger. He followed me as I jogged up the front steps and wrapped both arms around Birdie. I inhaled her aroma of coffee, bacon, and something sweet I couldn't identify but which made my mouth water with anticipation.

"I've missed you so much," I whispered. "I doubt I would have returned if you weren't here to welcome me."

She squeezed me back like she never planned to let me go. But she did, then held me at arm's length.

"Ha! That is absolutely ridiculous, Nikki Knight. You own this place, lock stock and barrel, and Audrey would haunt you forever if you didn't return and do it justice. And that, my dear girl, is exactly what you'll do. Come on in. You must have loads of tales to tell me about your trip. I have a hot cup of my special blend of knock-your-socks-off mocha cocoa waiting for you."

Then she stopped and gave me one of her evaluating looks, including an uplifted eyebrow. "Unless you prefer a regular cup of coffee."

Her scowl suggested that if I chose the boring option, she might just send me packing after she whipped some sense into me. Birdie only had time for the extra special things in life. She'd taught me not to waste a second on boring. If you're going to do something, do it up big or don't bother at all. I always wondered if she'd learned that from Audrey, or was it the other way around? I really didn't know. Sometimes, it was hard to tell where one of them ended and the other began.

My welcome was complete and whatever she'd cooked up for my arrival made my stomach grumble.

"You got a dog?" Birdie asked, finally noticing the four-legged guy tagging along with me.

"Oh. Him? Not mine. He found me when I stopped for gas. I plan to find his owner. After we eat."

Birdie never batted an eyelash about the mystery dog. She was used to me arriving with every size, shape, and color of rescued animal I'd stumbled upon.

She led the way to the kitchen. "We'll cross that bridge together," she said. "After you eat."

Fortunately, our priorities were in full alignment.

The dog didn't complain. He trotted along with his nose in the air like he had one goal in the whole world, and it didn't include finding his owner. He was most definitely intent on finding the source of the scent coming from Birdie's kitchen. I suspected he was looking forward to breakfast as much as I was.

After that? Maybe he'd worry about getting back to where he belonged.

He sure didn't seem too concerned, though.

## 2

I practically swooned at the sight and aroma of Birdie's spread on the well-loved maple kitchen table. She'd set a place right where I always sat, facing the window so I could watch the birds at the feeder. It was bittersweet, though, because of Audrey's empty seat next to me.

"Now, don't get all mopey, Nikki. You know Audrey wouldn't want you pining away over her. She'd tell you—"

"Put on a smile and get on with it," I said, finishing another one of Audrey's classic sayings. We both laughed. "But, I still miss her," I added defiantly.

Birdie hugged me. "Of course, you do, honey, but don't tell me you can't feel her right here with you because I know you'd be lying." She pulled out Audrey's chair and then sat in the one next to it. It was almost as if she expected our best friend to join us.

The dachshund sat next to me and looked up with an expectant gaze. I stabbed a sausage and dropped it on a plate, added a scoop of scrambled eggs, half a slice of buttered toast, and set it on the floor in front of him.

"There you go. A breakfast fit for a prince, right?"

He woofed a thank-you, or so it seemed. I expected him to dive in and inhale the food, but he didn't. Instead, he sniffed each item then decided on his course of action. The sausage disappeared first with one hearty bite.

With my guest occupied, I turned my attention to my own stomach and piled my plate with enough food to give me a stomachache. When it came to Birdie's gustatory creations, my eyes were always bigger than my stomach.

But, Birdie bit her tongue and didn't give any advice. She sipped her mocha cocoa and leaned back in her chair. It seemed like she was biding her time, waiting for me to stuff myself before jumping into whatever was on her mind.

I dug in like I hadn't eaten in a month. My four-legged guest licked his plate clean, and I was about to do the same with mine when Birdie's hand shot out, and she said, "No, you don't, Nikki. I might have tolerated that disgusting habit when you were six, but not anymore."

She pushed herself up and carried my plate to the sink. I transferred the few leftovers into a glass container for composting, snapped the lid, then sat down to enjoy my mug of cocoa like it was dessert.

"Delicious, Birdie. Thank you," I said and exhaled with satisfaction.

"You're welcome, and now you need to read this." She handed me an envelope.

I hadn't expected to receive mail so soon, at least nothing that she couldn't take care of, such as bills or junk for the recycling. "What is it?"

Birdie said nothing. She just stood next to me and waited.

I turned the envelope over, slid my nail under the flap, and popped it up. A single piece of paper folded inside slipped out.

I picked it up and read, "The Accidental Ghost?" then stared in confusion at Birdie.

"What is this?"

She sat down, reached across the table, and took my hands in hers. "There's really no easy way to explain, so I'll just dump it on you all at once." With that confusing announcement, she squeezed my hands, maybe so I couldn't leave. I wasn't sure.

"You know that your grandmother was murdered," she began and paused. I think the memory of that tragic day was as hard for her to talk about as it was for me to hear. "But what you don't know, Nikki, is that Audrey is still here in Moonlight Mansion."

I stared at Birdie. Had she completely lost it? I could understand if she had. Audrey and Birdie were as close as two people could be. Maybe she hadn't accepted the reality of the situation.

"She's a ghost," Birdie said, never taking her eyes off mine.

I flinched, but she held my hands in a vice-like grip.

She told me that after Audrey died, she found a book that she'd never seen in her upstairs apartment before.

"It seemed to have appeared out of thin air," Birdie said. "Like Audrey does now. Anyway," she nodded toward the paper in my hand, "you're looking at the first page of that book. I guess you'd call it the title page."

What the heck was she talking about?

The dog suddenly charged to the kitchen door. He barked with a ferocity of a lion ready to die while protecting us.

But no one was there.

I walked over and tried to calm him. "What is it, buddy?"

"My name isn't Buddy."

"Huh?" I looked at Birdie. "Did you say something?"

She shrugged and shook her head. "I didn't hear anything."

"Down here. It's me, Prince Dasher Dangerdog Bean, but I'll tell you this once: I only listen if you call me Dash."

I stared at the dog. This had to be a whacky hallucination brought on from being overtired from driving all night, and the stress of this new situation.

"Did you put something in my mocha cocoa, Birdie? I'm hearing voices."

"Oh, boy. Is Audrey talking to you?"

A cold breeze passed close to me, then a gauzy white form appeared.

I stumbled back to my chair and dropped like a stone onto the seat before my legs gave out.

The form hovered next to me, becoming more and more defined until I thought I was looking in a mirror. There, in front of me, was a vision of myself dressed in a flowy white gown. The same long, light brown hair and the same brilliant sapphire blue eyes stared right at me.

What was going on?

I closed my eyes and rubbed them, then opened them again only to see that this strange apparition was still staring at me.

At least the dachshund had stopped his infernal barking. He put his front paws on my legs. "You probably don't want to hear this, but you are the one and only person who understands me."

His lips didn't move like he was actually talking, but I heard words, and they had to be coming from somewhere. I shook my head like a dog attempting to rid himself of an irritating mosquito buzzing around in an attempt to dislodge this figment of my imagination.

The dog pawed at my legs. "Hey! Are you okay?"

Somehow, I understood him in a most bizarre kind of way. Or so it seemed.

And then a different but very familiar voice assaulted my ears. "Well, aren't you glad to see *me*?"

"Audrey?" I squeaked. Between seeing a ghost and communicating with a dog, I wasn't sure if I was in a nightmare or if my world had fallen into a third dimension. Or both.

"Don't look so alarmed, Niks. I taught you better than that. Now, tell me what the deal is with the dog."

Audrey became more and more visible, the dog continued to stare at me, and Birdie let out a great big snort.

"This is the best time I've had since you died, Audrey. The dog is a real bonus. Fill us in about him, Nikki," Birdie said.

She acted like nothing was particularly unusual, obviously enjoying this craziness. Me? I had no idea what I was feeling, but it wasn't joy.

"The thing is," Dash said, or thought, or somehow communicated with me, "I'm from the long line of royal Bean dachshunds."

I stared. Was I supposed to know about these royal dogs?

"But, to make a long story short, I got banished from my family for my shortcomings. I don't agree with the decision, but the rules are strict. So, here I am with my too-short legs —offense number one—and my power to communicate with one person. The royal Beans would never in a million decades tolerate that power."

"Why me?" I asked in a barely audible whisper. "You aren't just *any* person," he said like I should be honored with this newly found ability we shared. "*You* are descended from a ghost." With that announcement, he dropped back to the floor and found a few stray crumbs to clean up. Then, between licks, he said, "Tell your Birdie friend, she can cook sausage anytime—morning, noon, afternoon, midnight. They're my favorite."

Birdie got up and gave my cheek a gentle pat then sat back down

"You look like you just saw a ghost and heard an interesting story, Nikki. Oh right, you did see a ghost, and I can't wait to hear the dog's story since apparently, he shared something with you."

From the grin on her face, I could see that Birdie was taking everything in like it was just another day in the life at Moonlight Mansion.

What had I signed up for?

# 3

I explained to both Birdie and Audrey how I now had the unusual, and to be completely honest, extraordinary ability to communicate with one short-legged, ex-royalty dachshund. *If*, and in my mind, it was a gigantic if, he could be believed about anything, especially the royalty part.

Birdie almost choked up a lung from laughing so hard.

Audrey listened attentively, then said, "That will come in very handy with our new business."

I snorted out the last of my lukewarm mocha cocoa. "New business? Do I even want to know?"

"Oh, Niks," Audrey said. "You'll never be happy sitting around this big old mansion deadheading the flowers, although it is a therapeutic activity when you get old and have all the time in the world or baking peach pies, but Birdie has that under control. So," she emphasized, "of course, you need an exciting sideline. And," she paused, again only much longer, so I knew this next statement would be a doozy. "I've decided to become a detective, and I need a flesh and blood partner."

"A detective?" I said as if I'd never heard the word before. Of course, I knew what a detective was, but I knew nothing about *being* an actual living and breathing detective. I couldn't imagine how she'd come to this decision.

"Yup. If I have to be a ghost, I don't plan on just haunting houses and moping around forever. I plan to be a detective, the best ghost detective ever. Maybe even the only one, but that's beside the point. And, to be clear, I don't mean investigating other ghosts. My plan is to be a ghost with a talent for solving crimes."

It sounded interesting in a far-out, even spooky kind of way, but I wasn't sold on me being part of her whacky plan.

"But I have to run Moonlight Mansion," I whined like a teenager complaining about a ten o'clock curfew (which I'd done more times than I could count).

"Oh, phooey." A swish of air made my hair jump off the back of my neck. "You are the face of Moonlight Mansion, but Birdie runs it like a well-oiled John Deere tractor. Moonlight Mansion gives you the cover you'll need."

"Cover?"

"For detecting, Niks. Haven't you been listening? You can't very well hang up a detective shingle without the proper license and all that kind of malarkey." She swirled around the table as she spoke, the breeze ruffling Dash's ears. "But you can ask questions and maybe even do a little sneaky snooping if necessary, all while flying under the radar. Well I guess, I'll be the one flying under the radar. But that's beside the point. With your little four-legged friend at your side, he'll be able to inform you about every interesting scent undetected by the human nose, which gives you, my dear, a jump ahead of anyone else investigating."

It did sound intriguing, and sure, I'd been worried about boredom consuming me in Frog Hollow, but partnering with a ghost? Besides, what type of crimes were we even talking about? Missing kitties or lost wallets? That didn't sound very stimulating.

Audrey swished away from the table, sending the napkins fluttering into the air. I tried to grab them but missed a few. Dash sniffed them, probably hoping for more crumbs, but walked away without finding any treats.

"Don't worry. There's more going on in this town than you can imagine." Apparently, Audrey had read my thoughts. I'd have to be careful if this was another talent she possessed. Hopefully, it was just a lucky guess. Time would tell about that.

"I see and hear things I never knew about when I was a living soul. I even get a tingly sensation sometimes when something important is happening. I can't explain it, but it's exciting, Niks. Like goosebumps all over, in a good way. So, now that you're here, let's get started."

"Right now? I barely finished breakfast. Can I unpack first?"

"See, Birdie? I told you she'd come around, and it didn't even take much convincing." Audrey continued like this was our first business meeting with a win in her column.

"Fill her in on your first investigation plan," Birdie said. She sipped her mocha and settled in quite comfortably.

Audrey hovered next to me. "Okay. I've learned there's something shady happening in town. It sounds like some bad guys are getting organized to pull off a crime. My goal is to scare them away before they succeed in whatever they have planned. What do you think?"

It sounded awfully vague, but before I could answer, Dash nose-butted my calf. "Nikki, I need my bed. And my treats. And, a potty break," he demanded like someone used to getting exactly what he wanted.

I ignored his lack of manners because he might not be my problem for much longer. If Dash had a bed and treats stashed somewhere, he must have an owner.

"Where is your stuff?" I asked. Birdie looked at me with her eyebrows raised, but she didn't interrupt. Audrey stayed still also.

"In Vernon's car, of course," he answered like anyone with half a brain should know that detail.

"Vernon." I had a name! "Vernon is your person?"

"Don't be silly, Nikki. You're my person. Remember? I chose you, and I can't suddenly unchoose you."

"Unchoose is not a word," I said, not that it should matter to a dog. "And Vernon might feel differently about losing you."

Dash sat down. Was he thinking this over? I had no idea.

"If you say so, but the fact still remains that you are now my person. Vernon got me out of that dreadful jail where I had to sleep on a cement floor. The only plus was my very delightful jail mate. And I do miss her. Maybe you can spring her free. After we get my stuff, of course. I'm thankful for being out, but you'll just have to explain to Vernon that I'm moving in with you now. Don't I get a say in this matter?"

He had a point, but it didn't usually work that way. Since there was nothing normal about this morning, I stayed silent on that subject. I'd figure it out when I found Vernon.

Dash said, "So, when can we get my stuff?"

"You want me to tell Vernon that you've chosen me over him? What's this guy like?" I wanted every bit of info Dash could provide.

He cocked his head and tipped his ears forward. I tried to get mad at Dash to justify sending him packing, but I couldn't. Plus, he was more than adorable. And, I'd wager he was well aware of it, too.

"Like? He's taller than you and much heavier. He smells like nasty cigar smoke mixed with swamp, and he never gave me treats. I guess he's like a baboon. I can't even talk to him, so why would I want to live with him?"

I tapped my fingers on the table. Should I do the bidding of this dog who'd adopted me as his person? Or take care of my own needs. The thing was, taking care of Dash might ultimately help me in some crazy upside-down way as Audrey suggested. Plus, I couldn't deny that I was already quite attached to him. And best of all? I could talk to a dog! Never in my wildest dreams had I ever imagined something so fantastic.

I made a decision and explained it to my human and ghost companions. "Dash just informed me that he has a dog bed and treats in Vernon's car," I said, holding up my hands to Birdie and Audrey, so they didn't interrupt. "Don't ask because I don't know who Vernon is, but since it appears that Dash is moving in here with me... with us, I'm going to retrieve his things and try to explain the situation to this Vernon person. Who wants to tag along? I'm hoping Dash can help us find him."

"Go on an adventure with a dog giving directions?" Birdie said. "I wouldn't miss this adventure for the world."

"I'm in, too," Audrey said but without as much enthusiasm as Birdie. "It's a distraction from our detective mission, though. But I know when you've made up your mind, Niks, so let's get it done as quickly as possible so we can focus on the bad guys before they pull off their plan."

I guess I wouldn't be unpacking for a while.

## 4

I led the way outside. Dash took a detour to sprinkle on one of the lilac bushes first.

Birdie climbed into the back seat of my rental BMW, stashed her hold-everything-purse at her feet, and waited for Dash to join her. When I opened the door for Audrey, since I assumed she couldn't do it for herself, she was already draped over the passenger seat.

"What?" she asked, sounding perturbed. "You think I can't manage for myself?"

I should have known that she'd just float through the door, or through the window, or whatever she could do, but this ghost business was completely new to me. "I won't make the same mistake again," I assured her and climbed in behind the wheel.

The Georgia air had warmed and become a little steamy. This was probably a silly question, but I asked anyway. "Who wants the top down?"

"Woof!" Dash jumped up and down with the enthusiasm of a dog waiting for a yummy marrow bone. "If that's a thing, don't even ask, just do it," he said. "No more hanging my head out the window to smell everything? A dream come true. You should try it too, Nikki."

No thanks to the offer of riding with my head out the window. But I could understand the benefit from Dash's point of view. I'd probably be learning plenty from him as time went by.

With the top down, Dash balanced himself between the two front seats and stared straight ahead like a dignified statue, ready for anything as far as I could tell. Audrey, on the other hand, sank lower in the seat. Was she afraid she might blow away? I didn't dare ask and figured I would find out eventually.

"Here's the plan," I said as I left Moonlight Mansion and turned onto Live Oak Lane that connected us to Hoppin' John Highway. "I'll head to the spot where I found Dash. Then, it's up to him to smell the way to Vernon's car." Not a perfect plan, but it was all I had to work with.

We rode in silence for a few miles. My eyes feasted on the honey locust and loblolly pines whizzing by. Birdie sat like royalty next to Dash, looking left and right as we raced along.

Finally, from below the dashboard, Audrey broke the silence. "You never asked me how I know about the bad guys."

I glanced at her. Even in her shimmery appearance, I registered trouble. Her arms were crossed, and the pout on her face made her look like a sulky teenager.

"Sorry?" I said even though I didn't mean it. "I'm trying to get my head wrapped around a few little things that recently dropped in my lap like a series of exploding bombs." I glanced at her. "First, finding out that you're a ghost shocked me to my core, but that wasn't everything, was it? Add in the fact that I can now talk to a dachshund has my head spinning so fast I don't know if it will ever stop. And then you hit me up with being your partner in your detective shenanigans. I don't know the first thing about investigating. When you add everything together, I think it's fair to say that I've had an overwhelming morning."

There, I said what was on my mind, and the chips could fall wherever they wanted.

"But my breakfast feast made it all go down easier, right?" Birdie asked with proud confidence in her ability.

"Yes, Birdie. Your breakfast was exactly the fuel I needed. Thank you."

Audrey sat up a little straighter. "You're agreeing to be my partner?" Figures. She'd zeroed in on that part.

"Do I have a choice?" I smiled, then added, "Just kidding, Audrey. Of course, I'll be your partner. You're absolutely right that I need some excitement in my life, but your proposal came out of the blue, and I needed a little time for it to settle. So, tell me. How do you know about these bad guys?" If we were starting an investigation, I'd better get myself up to speed.

"One day, when I was a tad bored, I floated around town and checked out all the new shops. Since no one could see me, I stopped at a busy corner to listen to all the chatter," Audrey said, excitement back in her voice. "Niks, there's nothing like being invisible and eavesdropping."

I bet, I thought to myself.

"She got an earful, too," Birdie added.

"This one guy—about twenty-five, skinny, tattoos up and down his arms, and a gold front tooth—was bragging to another guy—probably in his fifties, overweight, bald, with a pasty complexion like he didn't get much sun."

"Maybe he's a ghost like you," I teased.

Audrey ignored my comment but continued with her

story. "Tattoo Guy said he needed help with some action. Bald Guy perked up, and Tattoo Guy said, 'Yeah, there's a good reward, too. Interested?' But Bald Guy hemmed and hawed. He wasn't biting without more information about the plan, which worked out great for me. Tattoo Guy told him, 'Nothin' dangerous. Easy money. that's all I'm sayin' for now.'"

"Stop! Stop! Stop! Stop! Stop!"

I slammed on the brakes, forgetting that Audrey and Birdie had no idea that Dash was screaming at me to stop.

Audrey oozed off the seat, ending up in a heap on the floor. Birdie's hand slammed against the back of my seat, and Dash slid forward, but instinctively, I shot my arm out and stopped him from crashing nose-first into the dashboard.

"Are you trying to kill us, Nikki?" Birdie asked, slightly out of breath from the ordeal.

"Sorry. Dash told me to stop."

"Vernon's car!" he said, his front paws now up on the dashboard, his tongue hanging out, and his ears perked forward.

"Okay, Dash. Calm down. I'll pull to the side of the road, but I don't see a car."

"Of course not." His nose went up. "I smell it with my superior smelling ability."

"How come Vernon's car is here? I picked you up a couple more miles up the road?"

"When he stopped at the stinky gas place, I smelled a bunny. Bunnies are a much more exciting scent, and I ran off to investigate. The bunny got away, which was okay since I really just needed to stretch my legs. Then, when I got back, the car was gone. I sat down to figure out what to do next, and then you stopped and let me in your car. My problem was solved."

It sounded like Vernon didn't care too much about Dash, which made it a whole lot easier to let him move in with me.

"There! There! There! Pull in! Pull in! There!"

Between Dash's excited woofs and loud commands, I got the point. I almost had a heart attack, too, from all the exclamation points.

Then I saw what he was shouting about. A sumac almost completely hiding a narrow pull-off at the side of the road. My car bumped over ruts in my attempt to squeeze as far off the road as possible. I flinched with every screech from each branch that scraped against the side of my beautiful red rental car. There, pulled in under a towering pine, I spotted a beat-up car which I assumed belonged to Vernon.

Dash jumped, flying up and over the windshield in a feat of impressive athleticism. His short legs propelled him across the hood, and another leap brought him to the ground. He ran to the mostly-hidden car, where he slowed enough to sniff around each tire. Satisfied with whatever he'd discovered, he moved to the closest tree, lifted his leg, and left his mark.

"What now?" Audrey asked. She was finally off the floor and more or less back to her normal, whatever that meant, state of dignified ghostliness.

"I'll check the car. If it's unlocked, I'll grab Dash's stuff, and we'll be out of here," I said. As far as I was concerned, the plan was simple. I certainly didn't want a confrontation with Vernon if I could avoid it."

Birdie beat me to Vernon's car and had already tried each door while I'd been talking to Audrey.

"Locked," she said. "But, don't worry. This car is old enough and I always carry my lock popping doohickey in my purse. It will get us inside in a flash." She must have registered my shocked expression. "What? I've locked myself out of my car more times than I want to admit, so I always carry it with me in case of an emergency. This, as far as I'm concerned, is an emergency, Nikki."

I wasn't about to argue, but I *was* shocked to learn that Birdie, who I'd always considered to be the most stable, law-abiding person in my life, was an expert locksmith.

What surprise would blind-side me next?

I didn't have to wait and wonder for long. Dash let out a long woo-woo-woo wail and took off into the underbrush.

Great.

"You follow him, Nikki. I'll take care of getting Dash's stuff out of the car," Birdie said, not taking her focus away from her tool as she carefully inserted the doohickey between the car's window and door frame.

Audrey said, "I'll stay with your car in case anyone stops. Don't worry. I'll scare them off if necessary." She raised her arms and swirled back and forth to demonstrate her spooky ability. I admitted it was effective.

This new situation wasn't ideal, but it was what it was.

I sighed and followed Prince Dasher Dangerdog Bean into the woods because I sure wasn't going to abandon him like Vernon did.

## 5

The dense underbrush slowed my progress to a crawl. Literally. I was on my hands and knees.

Dash's barking grew fainter. I panicked at the thought of losing him.

His barks stopped altogether. Then, in place of his frantic woofs, I heard Dash shout, "Nikki! Hurry!" His scratchy voice was more frightened than I'd heard yet.

I stopped for a second. Silence fell like a thick wall. No crackling of twigs, no birds chirping, not even any frogs croaking, only the sound of my heart thudding.

What now? I picked up my pace as much as possible, pushing branches and vines away from my face with both arms in a desperate attempt to find Dash. I had to trust my instincts that I was heading in the right direction and not going deeper and deeper until I was hopelessly lost.

I cupped my hands around my mouth. "Dash? Can you hear me?" I shouted, both frustrated and angry at him for taking off.

Nothing but silence. My stomach twisted into a giant knot. I'd barely gotten to know this adorable canine, and I couldn't bear the thought of losing him already. That was *not* an option.

"Dash!" I yelled, fraught with dread.

I heard a whimper. A thick barrier of branches blocked my movement, but I pushed, almost falling on my face when they finally broke apart.

In front of me, sprawled on the ground, his head hidden under a dark blue blanket which was practically hidden by leaves and brush, was my newfound friend.

"Dash?" I sounded pathetic to my own ears.

"Dash!" I shouted louder.

He wiggled backward, shook off an accumulation of leaves and twigs that covered his long body, then looked at me with bright eyes. A wave of relief swept through my body. I crouched down, prepared to sweep him into my arms, but before I managed to say anything, Dash said, "He's dead, Nikki."

I glanced around, but I couldn't see a body anywhere. Thankfully. What was he talking about?

"Who's dead?" For all I knew, Dash had found a dead chipmunk or mouse or some other woodland creature.

"Vernon. Under the blanket. It smells like blood and burning and nasty smoke and sweat and salt and dirt and cinnamon and... and so many smells. No accident there, Nikki. Nope. Someone took care of Vernon for good."

This was too much. I sank onto a nearby log and waited for Dash's words to sink in.

"And cat," he said as if it was a dirty word. "I smell cat everywhere. Different cats, too. Where are they?" Dash lifted his nose and sniffed the air, then dropped his nose to the ground. He methodically moved in ever-expanding circles as he sniffed. Fortunately, I gently but firmly grabbed his collar when he came close enough to me. I didn't plan to let him disappear trailing after another scent in these dense woods and risk losing him again.

My mind raced for a plan.

I put my hands on both sides of Dash's face and looked into his deep chocolate eyes. He stared back at me with all the trust I could ever imagine.

"We have to go back to the car, Dash. Do you understand?"

"But—"

"No buts, Dash. This is a serious situation. If you found a body, I have to call the police."

"You don't believe me." His whole body went limp.

"Of course, I believe you, but I don't want to touch anything." Or see a body. And I had to get Audrey home before she did something to make matters worse. I couldn't imagine what could be worse than stumbling on a body, but I couldn't rule out the unknown just because I hadn't imagined it yet. Lately, new surprises waited around every corner, ready to blindside me.

Dash blinked. It might have just been my imagination, but I thought I saw his eyes filling with tears. That wasn't possible, was it? Could dogs cry? Maybe a dog that could talk could cry. What did I know?

"You're right, Nikki. Back to the car. I'll lead the way so you don't get lost."

Apparently, he didn't have much faith in my navigational skills, but I didn't plan to argue with him. Time was at a premium.

"Hurry, Nikki. You don't want to get caught here with the body."

He was right. I shuddered and followed his long body as he easily wiggled through the underbrush while I was forced to slash at branches with my arms. Surprisingly, it was only a matter of minutes before he led me back to the car. It had felt like forever when I floundered around looking for him. Time was funny that way.

"Oh good, you two are back," Birdie said when I burst out of the dark woods into the open sunshine. "Let's get out of here before Vernon comes back."

"He's not coming back."

Birdie snorted. "What'd you do? Leave him tied to a tree or something? I suppose that would be poetic justice for abandoning Dash on the side of the road."

"Come on, Niks." I couldn't see Audrey, but I knew that stern, commanding voice better than I knew my own. "Birdie found lots of stuff in Vernon's car and stashed it in the trunk. That was my idea," she said proudly. "In case someone stopped, they wouldn't guess we did some serious looting. Now, we need to skedaddle home and sort through it all."

That did not make me feel any better, but before I could protest or tell them about Vernon's murder, Birdie pulled my arm and shoved me onto the driver's seat. She climbed into the back where Dash stood in his spot between the two front seats, his tongue hanging out and his tail wagging. Finding a body hadn't dampened his enthusiasm at all. I suppose that living in the moment described a dog's life to a T. And Dash's moment now entailed a ride in my convertible. My moment was all about getting as far away from this spot as possible before anyone saw us.

The branches that scraped the side of my car on the way in, did even more damage as I bumped over the ruts and backed out. Did I get the extra insurance? I couldn't remember, but if not, I was in for an expensive shock.

As soon as I drove away from the pull-off, Birdie leaned over the seat and asked, "So, Vernon? I hope you let him know that he'd never be seeing Dash again after what he did."

"No worries about that." I turned on my signal and made a left onto Hoppin' John Highway. "Vernon is dead."

Dash barked and added for my benefit, "As a dog bone."

Birdie wiped her hands together like she was cleaning off dirt. "That takes care of everything."

I silently disagreed.

"Nikki?" Dash said, his voice tentative. "Tell them about the cats."

"I don't understand what difference that makes. Cats didn't do it."

"You never know. Cats can be unpredictable."

I pulled into Moonlight Mansion's driveway, relieved to be back to what had always been my refuge. Unfortunately for me today, though, my refuge had been invaded by a police car. And, it was parked in my spot.

"That's nervy," Audrey said. "Officer Bud Brooksby parked in the spot that's clearly marked for the *owner* of Moonlight Mansion. I'm going to give him a piece of my mind."

"Audrey? No!" I reached out to grab her arm, but surprise, surprise, I got a handful of cold nothing. "You can't confront him. Let me go find out why he's here," I said.

"The body," Dash whispered nasally.

"Don't jump to conclusions," I snapped, then opened my door. I stepped out, gave myself a little pep talk, and put on a confident smile. One that I hoped said I'm in charge, *and* I have absolutely nothing to hide.

With as much self-assurance as I could muster, I walked toward Officer Brooksby even if talking to him was the last thing I wanted to do right now. I told myself there was nothing to worry about, except possibly the ghost, a dog I could talk to that I'd picked up at the local gas station, and a trunk full of who knew what that belonged to a dead man.

"Nikki, just so you know, he goes strictly by the book, and I never got along with him. There's a teeny tiny chance he might hold that against you," I heard Audrey say when I was almost next to the officer.

Great.

Anything else I should know?

6

"Officer Brooksby," the seventyish-year-old man announced, all stern and full of authority. "And you are?"

"Nikki Knight... Sir." I added the sir as an afterthought. It couldn't hurt to be respectful, right?

He smiled, but it didn't even reach halfway to his eyes. The kind of smile that wasn't really a smile at all but a preening display of authority. It was the kind of smile that said, this is my show, and you'd better follow my rules–the kind of smile I hated.

I prided myself on giving most people the benefit of the doubt. In this case, though, Brooksby left no doubt about who he was, and I didn't find one thing about him appealing, from his scuffed leather boots to his silver crew cut.

He looked past me, already a big black checkmark in his negative column, and so far, the positive column was empty.

"Ah, Birdie Bell Long," he said with fake syrupy sweetness. She stood next to me now. "And what have you ladies been up to?"

"Enjoying the Georgia morning in Nikki's convertible,"

Birdie replied in her best southern belle accent. I would have laughed if I wasn't about to wet myself. If he only knew what we'd been up to this morning.

"What brings you out here this fine morning, Brooksby?" she said, her cheery tone not giving anything away.

He scowled, which I could only assume was because she'd neglected to address him with his official title. Or maybe it was his normal expression.

"It's such a shame that Audrey isn't around to enjoy it, too," he said like he didn't mean it one bit. I had the feeling he hoped mentioning Audrey stung.

I felt a cold breeze swirl around us. It had to be Audrey giving Brooksby a dose of ghostly medicine. I wondered if she had enough self-control to keep herself invisible while she taunted him.

Birdie tucked a few strands of hair back behind her ears that the gust of wind had dislodged.

"There's a nice little breeze today," she said, managing to keep a straight face.

"If I didn't know better," Brooksby said with a nervous laugh, "I'd say this place is haunted."

Little did he know.

Dash finally managed to scramble his little body out of the car, landing with a thump. No graceful leap out this time. I'd hoped he would have stayed out of sight but no, he charged and barked at Brooksby. Not exactly helpful but it was funny to see the big man back a few paces away from the twenty-pound, and at best, eight-inch tall dachshund.

"Whose dog is this? I haven't seen him around here before. Is it yours, Ms. Knight?" Brooksby asked from his safe distance.

Uh-oh. Was that a trick question?

I picked up Dash and he wiggled and squirmed in my

arms. "Tell him, Nikki. Tell him I chose you. Tell him to get lost. He smells like someone you shouldn't trust."

"I had a report about a missing dachshund early this morning. Someone saw you stop and pick up a dog," Brooksby informed us. He stretched his hand out like he was about to pull Dash away from me but the little dog snapped and almost got a finger or two for a snack before Brooksby thought better of his plan.

"Actually," Birdie said coming to my rescue. "Nikki found this poor little dog abandoned. He was just sitting there, lost, forlorn, and hungry."

When she paused, I imagined sad violin music playing in the background.

"Of course, Nikki did what any caring individual would have done. She brought him home with her and fed him. I don't suppose you know who the owner is?"

"Yes, as a matter of fact, I do. The caller left his name and phone number. I have it someplace." Brooksby pulled out a beat-up three-by-five spiral notebook, took off a rubber band, and flipped it open. "Let me see," he mumbled as he scrolled through a few pages. "Yes. Here it is. A Mr. Vernon Quinn."

Dash tensed and barked ferociously like he was ready to charge again. His oversized personality certainly made up for his small stature.

Officer Brooksby studied Dash. "You recognize that name, little guy?"

"I'm not *little guy,* you big baboon. I do recognize that evil name, and if I could, I'd bite him for leaving me behind," Dash said. He snapped again at Brooksby even though he wasn't close enough to have a chance at doing any damage. His message was clear. At least to me.

Officer Brooksby paused and narrowed his eyes. Had he

understood Dash? I was so nervous that sweat poured down my side, completely soaking through the underarms of my white t-shirt.

But then Brooksby continued, "I'll call Mr. Quinn and let him know it appears his dog has been found. Of course, he'll have to show proof that he's the rightful owner."

"Of course," Birdie said.

"Good luck with getting ahold of him," Dash said and finally settled down in my arms.

I was so relieved I was the only one who could hear his commentary. Otherwise, I'd have some very uncomfortable explaining to do.

"Okay, then. We'll be inside," Birdie announced. "You just let us know when you connect with this Vernon guy. I do need to tell you, though," she waved her finger in Brooksby's face, "anyone who abandons an animal does *not* deserve to be reunited. It's irresponsible, unacceptable, and dangerous. This dog could have been hit by a car."

With that declaration, Birdie put her arm through mine and strolled up the walkway, pulling Dash and me along with her. I could have kissed her when she so cleverly extracted me away from the officer and any possibility of further grilling.

When we were safely inside with the door firmly shut behind us, I sagged against the wall. Audrey, however, hovered near the window, completely in her element as she narrated the play-by-play of Brooksby's actions.

"His phone is out. He's pacing. He shook his head and put it away," Audrey said from her vantage point. "I guess Vernon didn't answer. Big surprise, right?" She cackled like a foghorn. "Okay, now he's getting into his car. Niks? You're home free and clear." She pumped her shimmery fist in the air for emphasis.

I wasn't so sure.

"Until someone finds the body," Dash had to say, which didn't help my nerves one bit. He showed about as much concern for Vernon as someone who'd lost a penny. Sure, *he* didn't have to worry. That was all on me.

"Hey," he said. "Did you get my food from Vernon's car? That's what matters right now. My special blend of beef, rice, and carrots."

I rolled my eyes like we didn't have bigger worries than Dash's special food blend but informed Birdie of his concern.

"As soon as Brooksby's car is out of sight, we'll haul everything inside," she said, standing behind Audrey's glistening apparition. The two were still glued to the activity outside.

"Haul? What the heck did you take out of his car?" This couldn't be good.

Birdie waved her hand dismissively. "Oh, this and that."

"Whatever she could carry, Niks. Dash's dog bed, a bag of food, a briefcase, some papers, and a big sack. I would have helped, but you know, I can't actually lift anything anymore. Such a big shortcoming at times like this."

"Food? Did I hear someone say food?" Dash said. "Get my food before I die from starvation."

I'm sure he'd swoon at my feet right about now if that were remotely possible. I laughed at the absurdity. Dash was such a drama dog. I guessed he'd never been remotely close to starvation since not one rib showed through his sleek coat.

"If you've ever missed a meal, I'll run out and tell Officer Brooksby where to find Vernon's body," I said.

Dash actually made a noise that sounded like a harrumph.

"Niks?" Audrey said. "Speaking of bodies, did you actually see Vernon's?"

"No," I admitted doubtfully.

"How can you be sure it was him?"

I paused to remember the scene. "Well, I remember lots of brush, then Dash wiggled out from under a blanket and told me Vernon was dead." I held my arms out in a whatever gesture. "I believed him. Besides, I didn't want to look at anything gory."

She shot me a look. Well, a ghostly look. "You've got to be kidding. That's not proper detective behavior, you know. You should have looked at the body, gathered evidence, and found potential clues so we can figure out what happened. This could be the big break we need to get the detective agency off and running. We'll just have to go back," Audrey announced as if searching a murder scene was the equivalent of taking a walk out to her garden to feed her pet goldfish.

"What?"

It was barely noon, and my welcome to Moonlight Mansion should have been a relaxing, food-filled day. But no. Here I was with a ghost, a talking dog, and a murder investigation.

Birdie came in with an armful of stuff from my car and dumped it on the vestibule floor. She held up a small bag that looked like it had seen better days, or maybe it was just very well-loved. "You won't believe what's in this old leather pouch," she said.

I had no idea, but I did have a sinking feeling that it was another unwelcome surprise.

This day headed in the wrong direction as soon as I entered Frog Hollow.

My path went from terrible to far worse than anything I could have ever imagined.

# 7

Birdie unzipped the pouch and dumped a pile of shiny colorful gemstones into her hand. There had to be at least a dozen in all colors, shapes, and sizes.

"Woo-hoo!" Audrey hollered. "Maybe this connects to the bad guys."

I looked at the beautiful stones. To my untrained eye, I'd say rubies, sapphires, and diamonds. Could Audrey be right?

I thought about other possibilities, then snatched the pouch away from Birdie and held it down for Dash to take a look.

"Dash. Do you smell any clues on this?"

He sniffed, front, back, inside, and outside. "Cats. I keep telling you, Nikki, cats are at the bottom of this."

"What did he say?" Birdie and Audrey asked at the same time. Their impatience buzzed like an electric fence.

"Unfortunately, nothing helpful. He says it smells like cats. That only suggests that Vernon has cats."

"Or, his partner-in-crime has cats," Birdie said.

I tried to wrap my head around the cat business but got

nowhere. "Maybe Vernon's double-crossing partner murdered him."

At any rate, now we had the gemstones, which meant the murderer would be after us once he or she connected us to Vernon. I glanced at Dash. Was he the connection?

Audrey waved her arms and created a swirl of air in the vestibule. "Here's the plan," she said. "We have to hurry back to the scene of the crime before someone discovers Vernon's body and calls the police. Once they're on the scene, we'll never be able to snoop and gather any evidence. Then, we'll move onto step two."

"Which is?" I asked, not liking this step one at all.

"I don't know. We haven't gotten past step one yet. We have to find the clues first, Nikki, and then we'll know what to do." Audrey spoke like maybe I needed a brain transplant or something.

Or something was right.

As crazy as Audrey's plan was, I did see the very practical —and possibly life-saving—need for getting ahead of this situation. Once the killer discovered that we had the gemstones, we'd immediately become the next target. And when I say we, most likely it meant me because they couldn't go after Audrey. Time was ticking. These bad guys had to be stopped. At least what was left of them.

"The Underdog Animal Shelter will be our second stop," I said. "Because Dash told me that Vernon got him from a shelter, and that's right here in Frog Hollow. Someone there might remember something about Vernon."

"Yes, Nikki. Yes! My cage mate is there and lots of cats."

Hmmm. Interesting point.

So, without further discussion, I grabbed a handful of Dash's treats so he'd quit complaining about starving to death. Then we hustled outside to my scratched-up, red convertible BMW. At least Birdie had removed Vernon's loot from the trunk.

Birdie climbed in the back with Dash, who took up his position between the two front seats. I wasn't sure where Audrey was, but I heard a haunting whisper of doom in the car. It sounded sort of like, "You're next. Run. You're next. I'm after you."

"That's not helpful, Audrey," I said.

"You know, Niks, I have my special talents, and you have yours. I'm just practicing in case I have to scare anyone away from the scene of the crime. And since you didn't even think to investigate the scene when you had the opportunity, I'm not sure what your special talent is."

Right. I should have looked around, but hindsight is always twenty/twenty.

"I'm a thinker, Audrey. I try not to barrel straight into trouble without an escape plan."

That was true. Audrey had always been a spontaneous thrill seeker, and nothing had changed since she'd entered the afterlife. Or, maybe she was even worse. Don't get me wrong, I liked an adventure as much as anyone, but whenever possible, I didn't rush in blind. I wanted the facts before I made a move.

"That's good to know," Audrey said but I was sure, as much as she might try, she couldn't understand my style. If you're a "jump in with both feet" kind of person or ghost, you just can't live any other way.

"So, what's your escape plan?" she asked. "When the murderer discovers you have the gemstones, you'll be target numero uno. I can help, you know. I can scare the hair off a bald man if necessary. Just remember that when you find yourself in trouble."

I didn't answer. Not because I didn't have a plan, but

because I didn't want to feed her obsession. My plan was simple enough. I'd figure out what happened before the killer discovered we had the gemstones. Easy peasy and end of problem.

I started the car and pulled onto Live Oak Lane. Again. Driving helped me think, and the events were beginning to come together. In an abstract kind of way.

What I knew so far was that Vernon adopted Dash from the Underdog Animal Shelter, but since he left him at the gas station, he didn't seem to care much about him. Dash kept mentioning cats. Did Vernon go to the animal shelter for another reason but took Dash as a cover? A man traveling with a dog who stopped for walks wouldn't look suspicious. But it still didn't explain where the gemstones came from or why Vernon was killed.

"Slow down, Nikki! Slow down or you'll miss it!" Dash shouted.

I did slow down but not because I was about to miss the pull-off. There was no chance of that this time because a line of police vehicles had parked up and down the road and in the pull-off where we'd found Vernon's car. This was a terrible development.

"We're too late," Audrey said, obviously disappointed with this turn of events. "Drive past these cars. Dash and I can sneak through the woods. No one will see me, and who would pay much attention to a dog?"

Would that work?

Unfortunately, as I crept along and got next to the pull-off, Officer Brooksby stepped into the road and flagged me down. My heart skipped more than a couple of beats.

"Out for another drive, ladies?" he asked. Creepy fingers crawled up my spine when his beady eyes stared at me like he could see right through our plan. A smirk grew across his round face. This guy was trouble.

"That's exactly right, Brooksby," Birdie said from the back seat. I loved how she addressed him, but I didn't think it would help our situation one bit. "Nikki's been away from Frog Hollow for too long. She just can't get enough of driving in the fresh Georgia air. It makes you feel right at home, right, Nikki?"

I nodded. And smiled. And decided I'd like to kill Audrey for making this plan. The only problem was, she was already dead!

Brooksby lifted his cap and ran his hand over his silver crew cut. "Why are you sitting in the back, Birdie? Playing a little pretend game that Audrey is still with you girls today?" A deep evil laugh erupted from his belly.

As far as I was concerned, this guy should have his fingernails pulled out one by one.

I glanced at the passenger seat and realized it must look odd driving around with my only visible passengers in the back seat. Something I hadn't considered before and hadn't planned a good story to satisfy inquiring minds.

Birdie, though, with her quick comebacks, said, "Oh, you know, I want to keep the dog company. Plus, I love how the wind whispers through my hair back here. It makes me feel like a teenager again."

I didn't dare glance in the rearview mirror at her for fear of laughing.

"Oh, right, the dog. Tell me again where you found him?" Brooksby had his beady eyes on me again.

I waved my hand like it was nothing. "At the gas station. The poor guy was just sitting there," I said. "My heart broke as soon as I saw him."

Dash howled with a forlorn sound that would tug at anyone's heart. At least anyone not named Brooksby.

"You didn't get him from the owner? Because something is really strange here." Brooksby snapped his fingers. He tapped his cheek like he was trying to solve a puzzle while keeping us on the edge of our seats. "Maybe you can help me figure this out." Then, he turned and looked at Vernon's car, which had been pulled out from under the tree where we'd last seen it.

"Jane Cross at the Underdog Animal Shelter told me that before they let anyone adopt and leave with an animal, they have to have a bed, food, and collar. You said you found him on the side of the road. I see he has a collar but we didn't find a bed or food in Vernon's car. Strange, don't you think?"

"Food, Nikki. Food. Tell him you took the food," Dash said with a nudge under my arm.

"Very strange," Birdie agreed. "Maybe the shelter made an exception for Vernon?"

"Nope. Jane said she checked Vernon personally since that dachshund was a special case. Something about his bloodline, which I don't care about, so I didn't follow. At any rate, someone has the dog's stuff, and I'm sure you'll want it if you plan to keep the mutt."

"Mutt? He said mutt?" Dash leaped across my lap and barked at Brooksby with such ferocity the officer backed off. This was becoming a habit.

"I don't think he likes you, Officer," I said. Of course, any fool could have figured that out. "Maybe he's afraid you plan to take him back to the shelter. Once dogs get their freedom, there's no going back, you know."

"No, I don't know. I'm not a dog person. But I will warn you that he might end up back there because I have a sneaky suspicion you ladies know more than you're telling me. And if that's the case, that mutt won't be luxuriating at the Moonlight Mansion. If I don't get some answers soon, it'll be bye-bye, poochie."

Brooksby waved and walked off, laughing like someone who gets great pleasure from flaunting their power over others. I really, *really* didn't like him.

Then, he stopped and turned those squinty eyes back on me. "Those are quite the scratches on that pretty car of yours, Ms. Knight." He tapped two fingers to his forehead in a mock salute.

I reminded myself that this was a crime scene, and Brooksby was only doing his job. The disturbing part was that he looked at me like I was some kind of common criminal. He was suspicious, and rightly so, but that just pushed this situation into the red zone. It wasn't just the scratches on my red car that concerned me. Sure, they were a dead giveaway to any detective worth his weight that I might have been at this spot. But Brooksby had dropped a veiled threat at my feet, and there wasn't much I liked less than having a family member—which included Dash—threatened. This required immediate action. No matter what, I had to keep Dash safe, which might mean putting myself in danger, but so be it.

I had to find the killer before anything happened to my new four-legged friend. That was a promise.

Dash woofed, adding his unbridled approval like he knew what I was thinking.

# 8

I skedaddled from the crime scene without waiting for any dust to settle under my car, worried Brooksby might flag me down again and demand a lie detector test. I'd fail for sure.

Audrey hadn't made a peep in a dog's age. Definitely not like her.

"Audrey?" I said, my voice sounding like a Minnie Mouse squeak mixed with a heavy dose of worry.

By the time I'd driven beyond the investigation base area, I heard a whoosh, and an unmistakable cold breeze hit my face. By cold, I mean colder than the lowest air conditioning setting. It sent a shiver from my head to my toes.

"Birdie?" I said, shooting a side glance. "Was that Audrey?" I asked, more annoyed than worried. I didn't like my grandmother pulling a disappearing act on us. Even if she was a ghost.

And then suddenly, she announced, "I'm back," without a care in the world. "I'm right here next to you, Niks. Thanks for distracting Brooksby with your chit-chat. Great work. It gave me just enough time to check out the body. Boy, am I glad that I looked, even if I almost missed my ride home. You two won't believe what I figured out. Come on, Niks, pedal to the metal."

I stepped on the gas, happy to have an excuse to put the Beemer through its paces and get away from the gory scene that I had no interest in viewing–or even hearing about.

"Spare us the details, Audrey. My stomach can't take it," I said, feeling slightly queasy just thinking about dead Vernon.

"Oh, shoot. That was going to be the best part of my story." She laughed. "Just kidding. I couldn't believe that Vernon is, or was, the Bald Guy I heard talking with Tattoo Guy in town about some shady activity. That means Vernon, Dash, Tattoo Guy, and the murderer are all somehow interconnected. Isn't that a great discovery?"

"Great? Are you kidding? That puts us right in the middle of a crime, and from the tone of Brooksby's questions, he acts like he thinks we're involved."

"Not we, Niks, just you and Birdie. How can I be involved? He thinks I'm dead. That's the beauty of our partnership. A minor detail, at best."

I was glad she thought so because I wasn't ready to accept a fate like death for myself.

"The thing is," she continued, "I'm not dead and a goner, just dead and a ghost, which, it turns out, has some benefits I never anticipated."

"Enlighten us," Birdie said. I wasn't sure it was a good idea to encourage Audrey, but truth be told, I was sort of curious, too.

"Well," Audrey said in her best listen-carefully tone. "I'm sure you can imagine how useful it is to be invisible. Obviously, I can go anywhere and be that fly on the wall everyone would like to be at times. I mean, for me personally, I never actually wanted to be a fly, just the unnoticed intruder part. But, there's more. I hear every bit of chatter—confidential or not—that makes me privy to any clues that aren't made public. And," I think she raised her arm, but I wasn't positive, "I saw some odds and ends the police gathered: a matchbook, gum, a few of those gemstones and," she paused for what I assumed was the big finale, "the murder weapon."

"Me, too! Me, too!" Dash shouted. "Nikki, it was under the stinky cat blanket. A short, ugly metal thing that smelled like fire, and I hope I never see anything like it again."

I patted Dash. He whimpered a little, then calmed down.

"I'd just arrived when the police pulled the blanket away and, what do you know, there was Bald Guy like I already mentioned. Dead. No doubt about it. I suppose it's good you didn't look under the blanket, Niks, because you would have left evidence behind. But as a ghost, that's something I don't have to worry about."

I thought about Audrey's news. She didn't seem worried that I might be scarred for life after seeing Vernon's body, just that I'd leave my DNA behind. Sure, she was looking out for my future, but did she have her priorities straight?

With a reluctant nod to my future as a possible suspect, because I *had* been at the crime scene, I listed the facts we knew so far.

"So, Bald Guy is definitely Vernon. Vernon was shot and covered up with a blanket that, according to Dash, smells like cat. We took a pouch filled with gemstones from Vernon's car, and you saw some spilled near the body."

A thought just struck me, and not in a good way. "What if the killer was in such a hurry, he spilled some, then stashed the rest in Vernon's car because someone was coming?"

"Like us on our first trip looking for the place where you found Dash?" Birdie said. "Very possible and dangerous."

"And, that's exactly what worries me," I said. "The killer might know that we took the pouch and is watching and biding his or her time to strike."

"Fantastic deducting," Audrey said, her excitement bubbling out like a fountain in a desert oasis. "Niks, you're getting the hang of this detecting business. I knew we'd make a great team."

Of course, there was the teeny tiny detail that I'd need to stay alive long enough to solve the mess. Plus, if the killer was on to me and Birdie... yeah, not a pleasant thought in any shape or form.

"What do we do next?" Audrey asked. I was amazed at how casually she took the dangerous side of investigating this murder. Of course, she had nothing to worry about. She couldn't be murdered again. Whereas I had one precious life that I wanted to hang onto for many, many more years. I assumed Birdie felt the same way.

"I know what to do. Nikki, I know," Dash said. "We go to the animal place and look for cats."

That wasn't a bad idea, at least the going to the shelter part. Dash, though, had to stay as far away as possible. There was no sense in taking a chance that they'd insist on taking him back now that his adopter was dead. A shiver surged from my head to my toes. Dash had no choice but to stay out of sight as much as possible. I suspected he wouldn't like that plan.

"How about," I said, letting my ideas fall onto a list of bullet-points in my head. "Birdie and Dash stay at Moonlight Mansion. Someone has to be there to protect the gemstones. I'll go to the shelter for a look around."

I saw Birdie nod when I glanced in the rearview mirror.

Dash sighed and melted farther into my lap like he'd just been told he couldn't go on an exciting adventure. At least he didn't complain.

"I'll rustle up some meals for everyone since we need to eat, right Dash?" Birdie said, cleverly distracting him with his favorite subject.

He lifted his head off his paws and sniffed the air. "Eat? It's time to eat? Good idea."

I sent a silent thank you to Birdie.

"I'm going with you, Niks," Audrey said, and from her tone, I knew her decision was a done deal. She'd made up her mind, and that was that. It was a good idea, though. I liked the fact that she'd be with me. My invisible partner that no one but me could see or hear.

"Perfect," I said. "The plan is coming together."

It took me all morning to wrap my head around all this whacky and dangerous stuff. How could I have anticipated coming home to Moonlight Mansion to find my grandmother was a ghost, a talking dog had adopted me, and I'd fallen into a murder mystery in the course of a few hours?

I was itching to get to the bottom of this nightmare.

All I had to do was stay out of trouble and, more importantly, stay alive.

Easy peasy now that I had a plan and a ghost at my back.

## 9

I grilled Birdie about the Underdog Animal Shelter on our way back to Moonlight Mansion. I knew where it was, but I didn't know anything about the people working there.

Dash immediately figured out what I was talking about and butted in with a loud huff. "You're talking about that evil jail, aren't you? Where they keep dogs and cats in cages," he said, offering up his first-hand impression from his time at the shelter.

"Kennels, Dash, not cages. The shelter is housed in a grey, one-story building with lots of windows. It's not so bad. And the dogs and cats are only there until they're adopted," I told him.

He huffed. "*You* didn't have to stay in that cold, damp cement cage. I was yanked from the estate where I was used to having acres to roam around on freely until..."

He let out what sounded eerily like a human sob.

I couldn't hear the rest of his mumbling since he'd wiggled halfway onto my lap and burrowed his head between his paws. I wondered what he'd been through before I found him. I'd learned the talkative dachshund, normally, an open book on most subjects, used every opportunity to share his thoughts and opinions. So eventually, he might share more about his past when the memories weren't so painful.

He lifted his head enough so I could understand his gibberish. "One guy was nice to me," he said with a degree of fondness. "The rest of those people, though? Eh... okay I suppose for all the *normal* cats and dogs there, but don't forget, Nikki, I'm royalty. They couldn't provide the level of attention I, Prince Dasher Dangerdog Bean, was accustomed to, like my special diet, memory foam cushion, and filtered water."

It was abundantly clear that our new four-legged friend required some la-di-da luxuries or thought he did. If he didn't come to terms with his new situation, he might be disappointed living at the Moonlight Mansion, too. Sure, it was more than comfy but not equipped to cater to his lofty expectations. Dash would have to adjust. He'd have to fit in with *our* routine, not the other way around. Without any grumbling.

"Tell Birdie to find the secret recipe for my special dinner. It should be packed with the other stuff she took out of Vernon's car," he said as if giving instructions to a personal chef.

I relayed the message, and Birdie returned a big eye-roll in my direction. She had her routine, which didn't leave room for anyone to make demands, including an adorable dachshund. She loved to cook, but she said requests stifled her creative side. I wasn't about to argue with her. I'd learned ages ago it was best to stay out of her way and appreciate whatever ended up on her menu, but I wasn't sure Dash understood.

I changed the subject from Dash's dietary needs and brought the conversation back to the animal shelter. I wanted as much information as possible ahead of my visit.

"What do you know about Jane Cross?" I knew nothing about her except she'd taken charge of the shelter, renamed it the Underdog Animal Shelter, and seemed to get high marks for improving conditions.

"An unfriendly cow," Audrey said. "I don't know why she acted like I was less than a piece of gum stuck on her shoe when I was still alive. I was likable. Sure, I expected people to listen to me and follow my instructions, but that's because I always had a solid plan. And, I was a major donor. Jane tended toward wishy-washy and insisted that her way was the right way." Audrey threw both arms out in a ghostly version of whatever.

I coughed to hide a laugh. True, Audrey usually got along with people... if they did things her way. It wasn't that she was a tyrant. I decided many years ago that she just assumed she knew how to do everything better than anyone else. She was amazingly good at most things she did. But her need to be in control didn't always go over well. She never learned to slow down and just listen to the ideas of other people, to give them a chance. I'd learned to nod in agreement with her but then just go about my business. That strategy usually worked just fine and was much easier than getting into an argument.

Birdie leaned over the front seat.

"Maybe it wasn't you, Audrey. Jane gets along with animals better than with people. She puts all her energy into the shelter. As a matter of fact, when she took it over, the kennels were rusty and dirty. There weren't enough outside areas for the dogs. Then, she turned it completely around. Now? Everything is clean and spacious. She even added an inside/outside cattery with climbing structures and plenty of sunny sleeping areas. Jane's biggest problem is finding the money to pay her bills now that you aren't writing big checks for the animals. She's struggling with that. At least that's what I've heard through the grapevine."

"Okay," I said, calmer now. "I get the picture about Jane. She's an animal person and isn't great with people. I shouldn't expect her to welcome me with open arms. But if I make a donation, I might get a hint of a smile. How about the others that work there?"

I made myself a mental note to bring my checkbook. I had no problem using the money Audrey left me to continue to subsidize the animal shelter, no matter who was running it.

"Mostly volunteers, I think," Birdie said. "There are always new faces coming and going, except for one kid in his early twenties who's been there for a few years. He works in the back, cleaning the kennels. I've never spoken to him."

"Don't forget the nice guy, Nikki," Dash said. "He always gave me a treat."

It was good to know that I might find one friendly face that might lead to gaining some information. I hoped something would help me figure out who killed Vernon and why.

"He's the German shepherd," Dash said.

"Excuse me?"

"The nice guy. He's slow to warm up, but he's like a German shepherd—strong, handsome, big alert ears—you know what I mean."

It was a bit tiring repeating all his comments for Birdie and Audrey, but I did it anyway.

"Big ears, huh?" Audrey said. "Can't wait to see him. I'll bet all the women in Frog Hollow will be lined up outside the shelter hoping for a wink from him. Or maybe an ear wiggle."

She chortled her hollow-sounding laugh that was more like a distant foghorn than anything I'd ever heard before.

"Don't knock it," Dash said and plopped his head back on my lap.

"Dash?" I said, trying to decide if I should ask him what I was thinking or leave my curiosity unanswered.

"Yes, Nikki. If you're wondering, I've got you tagged as a golden retriever: loyal, beautiful, and intelligent. I saw it as soon as you crouched down and let me sniff your hand."

I was floored by Dash's insight. He saw everyone as a type of dog? I supposed that made sense in a canine kind of way.

"I'm a golden retriever," I informed the other two.

"What about me?" Birdie asked, jumping into this new game. "Ask Dash what kind of dog I am."

I asked but already had her pegged as a pit bull.

"That's easy. Birdie is a dachshund like me."

I told Birdie what Dash said and wondered what she'd think.

"I suppose that my legs *are* kind of short," she said, getting laughs from Audrey and me. But I wasn't sure it was meant as a joke.

"No. No. No. Not that part," Dash said. "Birdie is loyal and courageous. The two of us together are double the trouble for anyone thinking about sneaking around unwanted. The best part is that people won't expect much from either of us."

I laughed out loud at the vision of Dash and Birdie sneaking around together and told her what Dash had said.

. . .

"Now, that I like." Birdie had a satisfied grin and proud tilt of her head when I looked in the rearview mirror. "Watch out, everyone because the Birdie/Dash duo will be on guard at Moonlight Mansion."

"And, me?" Audrey said. "Just because I'm a ghost doesn't mean I can't be part of this game."

"How about Audrey? What kind of dog is she?" I asked Dash.

"Not a dog at all. Audrey's a cat. Her impulsive and dominant streaks, plus her tendency to come and go on her own schedule, is cat-like behavior. This is fun," he added.

Audrey hissed then yowled. She sounded exactly like an angry cat. "I might as well practice the sound effects that go with my part," she said.

Dash looked up at me like he wanted a pat on the head for a job well done.

I obliged. He'd hit the nail on the head with all of us.

Now, I wondered about the guy with the German shepherd personality at the animal shelter. Was Dash right about him, too?

## 10

When I dropped Birdie and Dash off at Moonlight Mansion, I ran inside, too. I grabbed my shoulder bag, stuffed my checkbook inside, added a water bottle and a couple of my favorite granola bars Birdie had stocked just for me—oats and nuts covered in a thick layer of dark chocolate. My emergency stash for any unexpected delays.

I also made an overdue stop in the powder room just inside the front vestibule.

"Now I'm ready for anything," I said on my way back to the Beemer. The flashy return into Frog Hollow that I'd planned was derailed. Instead, everyone had probably heard that Nikki Knight was back in town, in trouble with the police, and sticking her nose where it didn't belong.

If that were the case, I'd be sure no one was disappointed with my activities.

"A cat, huh?" Audrey said as soon as I'd started driving. "And what kind of cat would that be, pray tell?"

"Dash didn't specify, did he? Besides, what difference does it make? Cats are cuddly, smart, and graceful." I left out, bossy, aloof, and opinionated to avoid starting an argument.

"A big difference," Audrey said like her whole ghostly future hinged on my answer. "There are the adventurous types and the laid-back types. So, which am I, Niks?"

Oh, boy. This was a loaded question if I'd ever heard one. What if I made the wrong choice? The last thing I needed right now was to distract, and possibly upset Audrey when I needed her to be clear-headed. I thought fast. If I was a cat, which breed would I want to be?

"A tabby cat," I said.

"That just refers to the coat pattern on many different breeds, Niks."

Darn. She was really putting me on the spot. "Okay, Audrey. First and foremost, you're curious. You also love to give your opinion on everything, so you're a talker, too. You're smart, active, and don't like to be left out. Last but not least." I glanced at her to see if she was paying attention. She was. "You've proven that you have more than one life. Time will tell if it's nine like a cat has."

"All true," she said proudly. "So?"

"In my opinion, all those traits add up to a Bengal cat. And, you know what some people think about Bengal cats?"

"They're gorgeous?"

"Yes, but that's not what I was going to say. Some people think that Bengal cats are like dogs so you possess the best of both worlds, Audrey." Would she buy it?

She clapped her hands together, although there was no sound, just a slight breeze.

"I knew it!" she said, the delighted owner of an acceptable new title.

I wasn't sure what she thought she knew, and I wasn't

going to ask. As far as I was concerned, I'd dodged a bullet with that subject and was ready to move on.

"So, Jane Cross?" I stared at my grandmother. "You two didn't see eye to eye?"

"Jane was always happy to take my money but..."

"She didn't thank you?" I'd be miffed about that, too.

"No, not that exactly. She always sent out a nice thank you card from the dogs and cats featuring the latest adoptee. The cards were well-done."

"But?"

"But it felt impersonal." Audrey paused, and I thought, end of subject, but then she continued. "I suppose I expected her to be happy to see me, gush over my help in person, that sort of thing. Apparently, that wasn't her nature."

And now it was too late for Jane to let Audrey know how much she appreciated the donations. The money must have meant a lot since it allowed her to do so much for the animals. If Jane was struggling to pay her bills now, was it possible for her to change her strategy a little? Learn how to make the donors feel special? It shouldn't be so hard. Maybe she just needed some guidance.

"Do you know who Dash was referring to when he described the guy who's like a German shepherd?" I asked.

Audrey didn't answer. I couldn't see or hear her and wondered what she was up to.

"Audrey? Still here with me?"

"I'm here. I'm still thinking about your question. You know, Niks. Sometimes it's better to go into a situation without any preconceived notions."

That was an evasive answer that didn't sit well at all. "You do know the guy?" I said again. "Tell me who he is.

Since he doesn't know me from a hole in the ground, give me something, so I have the upper hand."

I heard a long, slow hiss of air from the seat next to me. Exasperation?

"Okay. I think Dash was referring to Will. He volunteers at the shelter. He hasn't been living here for too long. He's very good-looking if you like the preppy look: khakis with a leather belt, button-down shirt, neat haircut. I think he went to school at one of those hoity-toity schools in New England, although I never noticed an attitude from him. He's smart, and he works hard. If he was a dog, I agree with Dash, he's definitely a German shepherd."

"He sounds perfect, but..." I was excited to meet Mr. Nice Guy, who loves animals. "So, now tell me what's wrong with him?"

Audrey looked away before she said, "His last name is Brooksby."

I slammed on the brakes so hard I locked the wheels and almost skidded off the road. "Brooksby? As in related to Officer Bud Brooksby, who looks at me like I'm a murderer? You've got to be kidding."

"His grandson. I warned you, Niks. I said it might be better to meet him without all this background information. But, now you know. Just remember that Will works at the animal shelter, so that's a big positive. His grandfather doesn't even like dogs, so maybe they're complete opposites."

"Like Will the German shepherd and Bud the what? A flea?"

Audrey laughed so hard it came out like a long wheeze. "Or, maybe a swamp creature from the lagoon. Someone who rises from the muck when there's trouble and then crawls under the nearest rock after we sort out the mystery."

I thought about the serious bit she'd just implied beneath her amusing imagery. "You really think we can solve this mystery?" I knew I had doubts.

"Of course, I think you can, Niks, and you will. With my help." Her soft, tender tone made me choke up a little. "You can do anything you set your mind to. I've always said that, and I still believe it. Have faith in yourself, but don't be afraid to ask for help. Even if that help comes from an unlikely place."

What was that supposed to mean? Was she suggesting Will Brooksby might be able to help me? I wasn't sure I wanted to encourage a friendship that would put me in his grandfather's crosshairs. No thanks.

I'd find out soon enough, though, since we'd arrived at the fork on Leafy Lane that took us to the Underdog Animal Shelter.

I pulled into the parking lot and parked next to an old Volvo station wagon. An old pock-marked pickup truck and a blue motorcycle pulled in where I could barely see it were in the lot. The shelter itself was nestled among a thicket of trees that created lots of shade.

As soon as I heard the racket of dogs barking, people talking, and cats meowing coming from inside, I thought about Dash. When he ended up in a place so opposite from what he was used to, he must have thought he was having a nightmare. If I was honest with myself, even at the best shelter, the animals were scared and lonely. I decided that I'd give Jane every benefit of the doubt. Regardless of her personality defects, she was helping these animals.

"Before you go inside, Niks," Audrey said. "Banish me from your thoughts. You don't need the distraction. All you need to know is that I plan to snoop around and see what I can uncover, but I'll still keep an eye on you. Just in case." In case of what she didn't say, and I didn't ask.

"I want to find out more about the guy Birdie mentioned. The one who works in the back. Something tells me he might be an important link to Dash and Vernon."

I grabbed my shoulder bag and a huge helping of confidence. I'd need it.

Then, I headed to the entrance.

## 11

I'd almost reached the door of the animal shelter when I heard angry shouting coming from inside.

"I have to find him, and that's final!"

The door opened, and a rather large woman with droopy eyes rushed out on a dangerous path straight toward me. I jumped to one side, barely avoiding impact. At first glance, she reminded me of a Saint Bernard. The only thing missing was a whiskey casket tied under her chin.

*Thanks, Dash, now, I'm seeing people as if they're a dog.*

"Oh, sorry," the woman said. "I'm a bit distracted."

Her employee tag ID'd her as Jane Cross, so I held out my hand.

"Nikki Knight," I said. "I've just moved to Frog Hollow, and this is one of the first places I wanted to visit. My grandmother, Audrey Knight Fernsby, was always a big supporter of your shelter."

There, it sounded plausible, plus I'd laid an opening at Jane's feet. All she had to do was pick it up and go with it to express her undying thanks to my deceased grandmother. Simple. Or, so I thought.

"Yes. Well, I'm in a bit of a rush. Can't chat," she said, obviously flustered. She darted along the path to the old Volvo, slid inside, and slammed the door like she couldn't rid herself of me quickly enough.

Her surprise brushoff stung.

"I told you. Good luck getting any info from that one," Audrey whispered near my ear. "Next time, show up in a golden retriever costume. Maybe then she'll give you a pat on the head at least."

Leave it to Audrey to offer a ridiculous solution. I tried to keep a straight face, but a snort snuck out.

"Toodle-oo," Audrey said. She followed her goodbye with a whoosh of air that swirled like a cyclone before it disappeared around the side of the building. It sure seemed like she had the easy job in this partnership.

I hadn't even set one foot inside yet, and my defensive shield was beginning to squeeze the air out of my lungs. I took deep, cleansing breaths. In slowly and out slowly as I counted to ten. Complete calmness didn't envelope me, but I was focused and ready to face my next move.

I walked into the Underdog Animal Shelter, and right off the bat noticed the antiseptic aroma that mostly masked kitty litter box and dog kennel smells. It wasn't bad, but I wouldn't want to live in a crowded animal house.

"Can I help you?"

I noticed the young man sitting at the desk surrounded by cat crates stacked at least three high. He didn't look exactly like a German shepherd, though. He didn't have upright alert ears, but I had to agree with Dash. The guy oozed the confidence of a shepherd under a very handsome exterior. His dark brown eyes seemed to assess me with expert knowledge of body language.

I immediately felt self-conscious under his appraisal. I

licked the corner of my mouth in case I'd left a smear of chocolate from gobbling down a granola bar in the car. I pushed stray hair away from my face. Now, I wished I'd spent more time getting cleaned up this morning after my long trip. But who knew I'd be standing here in front of this guy dressed in a well-fitted t-shirt that strained against his broad shoulders with a charming smile on his face.

Nothing to do about my looks now but smile. Awkwardly.

"Hi," I said. "Is this the Underdog Animal Shelter?"

Did I really just ask such a dumb question?

But the young man, who I noticed from his name tag was in fact, Will Brooksby, smiled back at me and leaned back in his chair. "Yes, ma'am. Can I help you?"

Ma'am? How old did he think I was? I was definitely younger than him. I had to pull myself away from my raging hormones and get this visit under control. And fast.

I stepped toward him with my hand out. "Nikki Knight," I said. "I'm wondering if I can ask you a few questions."

His lips twitched. His eyebrows made a lightning-quick up and down wiggle. Did he find me amusing?

"Go right ahead, Ms. Knight. I presume you have questions about our adoptable animals or maybe you'd like to volunteer? We're always looking for more help."

I walked over to the stack of crates behind him. The black kitty inside the top crate made a lot of noise, so I stuck my fingers through the bars to give it some attention. "I'm wondering about your adoption procedure."

Will stood up and opened the crate, plopping the big cat in my arms. "It's pretty simple. You fall for one of our furry friends, get all the necessary items you'll need to make him or her comfortable at your home, pay the fee, and that's about it. Are you looking for a cat? Because that one told me he wants to go home with you."

"The cats talk to you?" I asked, totally dumbfounded. Could he actually talk to cats like I could talk to Dash?

Will let out a loud belly laugh. "I haven't exactly reached that level of communication yet, but Midnight seems smitten with you, Ms. Knight."

Smitten? What guy actually uses that word?

By now, Midnight was head-butting my chin and purring so loudly he could win a spot in the local band.

"Midnight is quite the lover. He won't last long here. The shy ones are harder to place."

"Oh, I'm not quite ready to adopt. I have a cat already." Technically, Mocha, the resident Moonlight Mansion kitty, belonged to Audrey, and I hadn't even seen him yet, but I assumed he was still around. With Dash in the house, he'd probably decided to make himself scarce until he'd assessed the new intruder.

And, I'd almost forgotten that I had a dog too, but I'd have to discuss that detail delicately.

"Maybe one of our dogs, then? You strike me as a good match for a golden retriever mix we have who is waiting for her forever home. Should I bring her out?"

"Why a golden retriever?" I had to ask.

He smiled at me. I didn't want to like this Will Brooksby guy, but that smile set all my nerve endings tingling.

"Well, this particular dog is a sweetheart and easy going, but she's not doing well here in the shelter. She could be a good match with you, Ms. Nikki Knight. Honey is slow to warm up, but once she does, she's eager to please."

This meeting was not going in the direction I'd hoped. I needed information from him, not a sales pitch for a dog, even if she did sound special. The fact was, his chatter or possibly flirting—I wasn't sure—was making me uneasy.

"Your questions, Ms. Knight?" Will sat down and leaned back comfortably in his rolling armchair. He seemed to be enjoying this way too much. He stretched out his long legs and crossed his ankles, presenting the classic easygoing image.

Me? I distracted myself with Midnight, who'd settled into my arms like he never wanted to be anywhere else.

My question, Mr. Brooksby..."

"Will," he interrupted and snapped himself upright. "Mr. Brooksby is my grandfather, Officer Bud Brooksby actually, and I don't care to be mistaken for him," he said with all the joking banter quickly gone from his tone.

Interesting. This was the first crack he showed in his otherwise mellow demeanor. This short but angry outburst suggested a problem between grandfather and grandson. I couldn't say I was surprised. From what I'd seen so far, Officer Brooksby was not particularly likable.

"Okay... Will. I heard," I paused as I gathered my thoughts to make sure that everything I said was common knowledge, "about a man who was murdered here in Frog Hollow. And, I heard that he..."

"Adopted a dog from us?" Will interrupted again. His tendency to finish other people's thoughts was off-putting, but this time it made my life easier.

Will stood up again, his chair snapping back, and moved in front of me so quickly I wasn't sure how he got there. "Where did you hear that?" he asked. His tone was controlled, so I wasn't sure if he was upset by my question or simply curious.

"Your grandfather, actually. I was... um... driving with

my friend earlier and happened by the scene of the crime. Your grandfather flagged me down and wondered about the dachshund in my car. I'd found him at the gas station and had no idea who he belonged to."

"Really?" he said. Will towered over me in his form-fitting black t-shirt, shaggy, light brown hair, and scruffy beard. It was the opposite of the preppy look Audrey had described.

"We need him back. Jane ran off in a huff to look for Prince Dasher. You have him now? That's why you're here?" His excitement made him ramble from one thought to another.

"No. I don't have him here, and you can't have him back. But, I can assure you that he's safe and very happy with me."

I couldn't very well tell Will that Prince Dasher Dangerdog Bean had chosen to live with me. The one person descended from a ghost who he'd decided was the only person able to communicate with him. An impossible situation to explain. Will would think I'd lost my mind.

I handed Midnight to Will, ready to make my escape before things went downhill from here.

While Will was distracted getting Midnight back in his crate, Audrey whispered in my ear. "Tattoo Guy is here. He's the guy Birdie said works in the back. I just heard him on the phone, telling someone the gemstones are worthless, and he didn't sound happy. You have to make an excuse to go in the back, Niks."

Geez, Louise. Now?

"Um, Will?" I said. "I changed my mind. I would like to meet that golden retriever you mentioned."

His face lit up like a full moon. "You won't regret it," he said.

Somehow, I knew I would.
"I'll bring Honey out."
"I'll go back with you."
What the heck was I doing?

## 12

Will led the way between the cat crates and piles of blankets and put his hand on a swinging door. I eyed the sign that said STOP UNLESS ACCOMPANIED BY AN EMPLOYEE. He paused as if he was weighing something important. Then, before he pushed the door open, he said, "Most people don't want to come back here. They prefer to meet a dog away from the reality of the kennels. It can be upsetting, Nikki. The dogs look at you, and their eyes plead for attention, for a home away from all the barking. They get really excited when new people visit."

I nodded, acknowledging the warning, and braced myself as I followed Will through the swinging door. Deep barks, high yips, and everything in between assaulted my ears. My heart broke a little with each kennel we passed. I wished I could bring every single pup home. Since that wasn't possible, I promised myself I'd help these dogs with a donation and my time. But, for now, I needed to get information.

"Honey's in a different wing where we put the shy dogs.

It's quieter, and she's more comfortable there." He pushed through another door, which closed behind us and muffled the barking.

Will stopped in front of a kennel. "Here we are. Come here, Honey. You have a visitor," he said in a soft, cheerful voice that gently caressed my ears and Honey's too, probably.

Honey came to the kennel's door, wagging her tail and looking at Will with expressive eyes that were deep pools of emotion. She was smallish, maybe only forty or forty-five pounds. But beautiful with rich strawberry blonde fur that was only a tad lighter than my own hair with the same thickness and waves.

"We think she has some poodle mixed in. Not sure, but she is smart as a whip. Right, Honey-poo?"

"Honey-poo?"

Red crept up Will's neck and spread across his face. "That's what Jane calls her. We think she had a bad experience with someone shouting at her. Loud noises make her tremble, but I'm hopeful that once she's adopted, she'll adjust and become a strong, confident girl. We also think a female should adopt her," he added with a suggestive tilt of his head toward me.

"No pressure, though, right?" I said, suspecting that was exactly his goal and wanting to let him know I saw through his gesture. I also knew that every minute I spent with her would make it harder to walk away.

"How about I put her on a leash, and we take her out into the yard. That way, you can see how much she loves to play."

I nodded and looked around. "You don't have anyone else helping you here?" I asked. So far, I hadn't seen hide nor hair of Tattoo Guy.

Will rolled his eyes. "There is a guy, Clive Martin. He's worked here for about six months, and he can do no wrong in Jane's eyes. Since it's her shelter, she makes the decisions, so I put up with Clive as best as I can. He's probably out having a cigarette, which is totally against the rules, but," Will shrugged like there was nothing he could do about it, "Jane is out, and it is what it is. I don't plan on letting a punk like Clive drive me away from the animals, though. It's all about the animals as far as I'm concerned."

When Will opened Honey's kennel door, she immediately sat down, politely waiting for him to snap on the leash. My heart melted a little more with every minute I was with this sweet girl.

"The door outside for this wing is that way," he said and pointed to a red EXIT sign. "Each wing has its own exit into the big fenced-in area for the dogs to play in when visitors or volunteers visit. It's really the highlight of their day."

I didn't doubt that. On our way to the exit, we passed a few more kennels with dogs curled up in baskets or sitting quietly. Every kennel was spotless. If that was Clive's job, at least he did it well.

"Hey! Willie!"

I turned around and saw a scrawny guy with his t-shirt sleeves rolled up, exposing arms covered with tattoos. He stood just inside the door we'd come through. Light glinted off his gold tooth when he grinned, a sneery kind of expression. It had to be Clive, aka Audrey's Tattoo Guy.

"Shouldn't you be up front in case a visitor comes?" Tattoo Guy said like he was running the show.

I heard a bell ding-dong.

Tattoo Guy snorted. "I must have that ESP thing."

"Don't worry about it, Clive. Since I haven't figured out how to be in two places at the same time, I'll get that as soon as I take care of this visitor. She's taking Honey outside," Will said. An unmistakable edge laced his voice.

"Yeah? Who's the babe with ya now? She the one who has that hound, Prince Something-or-other Bean?" he snickered when he said Dash's name.

My blood ran cold. How could he know that I had Dash unless he'd seen me stop and pick him up?

"Shouldn't you mind your own business and finish cleaning the kennels?" Will said. He took my arm and led Honey and me outside. "Sorry about him," he muttered. "Kind of a jerk and no manners. He can say some totally inappropriate things."

"Why does Jane put up with him?"

"She really doesn't like people to know this," he paused like he wasn't sure he should tell me this tidbit, "but he's related somehow." Will shrugged again like this explained everything. I suppose it did to a certain degree.

"Jane doesn't like Clive to interact with visitors, though. I guess you can figure out why. Visitors are my responsibility." He turned and smiled at me. A real smile that reached the corners of his eyes and made me wonder if I could trust him even if his grandfather acted like I might be a criminal.

The door thudded closed behind us, and Will unclipped Honey's leash. She charged around the enclosure like she hadn't had a chance to run for ages. Will picked up a tennis ball and threw it across the yard. Honey raced after it so fast, she caught it before it hit the ground.

"She's tough to trick and usually catches the ball in the air, but if not, she gets it on the first bounce. Every time," he said and handed me another ball. "I have to go back inside, but you can stay out here with her as long as you like."

"Will?" I had to get something off my chest. "What's the big deal about the dachshund? Isn't the important thing that he has a good home, regardless of whether he's with the original adopter or not?"

He paused with his hand on the door. "I wish I knew. There must be something special about that dog, but I sure wasn't kept in the loop. Jane handled all the paperwork. And, the weirdest thing was that no one ever came to actually visit him. Yesterday, that Vernon guy showed up, and boom, Prince Dasher was gone." He walked back next to me and whispered. "To be honest, I'm glad he's with you and not with Vernon and not back here."

"Did you meet Vernon?"

Will shook his head. "Not in any formal way. I saw him go out here with Clive, but I don't know what they were doing. It was unusual, for sure. Everything about Prince Dasher was strange, from the day he arrived to the day Vernon picked him up."

"Who brought him here?" I asked. That could lead to more information about his background.

"Jane brought him. She said she got a call to pick up the dog. Never told me from who, and that's all I know." Will's bottom lip jutted out, almost like he might shed a tear or two.

Getting information from Jane was probably a dead end considering the one interaction I'd already had with her. But, and this was big, I had Prince Dasher Dangerdog Bean and that just might get Jane to warm up to me.

I felt Audrey's cold presence next to me. It was comforting in a bizarre kind of way.

"Ask Will about the bad guys," she whispered.

"Will? Can I ask you one more thing?" I said before he'd disappeared inside.

"Yeah?"

Then another ding-dong sounded.

Will huffed like he was frustrated. "Sorry. I gotta see who's here," he said and disappeared back inside.

I was alone with Honey, which was just fine by me. I fluffed her soft ears when she sat next to me. "You're a sweet girl, aren't you?"

She didn't answer, not that I expected her to, but she did look at me with trusting eyes. Eyes that begged me to give her more than an occasional visit.

"We'll see," I said and meant it.

"She's a beauty, Niks," Audrey said. "There's room at the mansion for another dog."

I turned around but saw nothing except a slight wisp of white.

"Yeah, that's what I was thinking, too. I wonder what Dash would say if I bring Honey home." Was I really worried about his opinion on this matter? Not worried, just curious because I realized that I had made up my mind.

Audrey whispered, "Head's up. Jane's on her way out here, and if I sense anything, she's on a mission. And not a pretty one."

A door to the yard opened with such force it slammed into the wall with a loud bang. I jumped. That door was not the one I'd gone through. It must lead from the other wing.

Jane, at least five foot eight if I had to guess, was dressed for physical work in jeans, a t-shirt, and boots. Her long brown hair was tied in a ponytail and pulled through the hole in the back of her baseball cap. She glared at me with nostrils flaring and barely contained anger steaming from every pore.

Honey charged straight to her.

I stayed where I was.

Audrey totally ghosted me, which gave a second meaning to the word. At least, in her situation.

*Scents and a Suspect* 77

"You have Prince Dasher," Jane said, not a question but a statement filled with resentment. She scowled. "You didn't tell me when you arrived an hour ago, which means I just wasted that hour hunting down Officer Brooksby only to find out you had the answer to my question."

Her sharp, nasal voice almost made me run for cover. But of course, I didn't. I squared my shoulders in a show of strength and confidence. She was *not* going to intimidate me.

At least I wouldn't show it.

## 13

"Well?" Jane asked.

I wasn't sure what the question was, so I waited for her to show her hand.

Her shoulders raised, and she let out a loud huff. Her fingers sought Honey's soft fur, and the contact seemed to absorb a tiny bit of her bluster. Or was that just wishful thinking?

She looked around the yard. "Where's Will? I assumed he'd be out here exercising the dogs."

That was a question I could answer. "Will was the perfect host when I arrived," I said. Praising Will seemed like a good idea. "He brought Honey and me out here but went back to the office when the bell rang. He said I could stay as long as I wanted to."

"He wasn't in the office." She sounded like somehow it was my fault. I had a bad feeling that this relationship with Jane, which had gotten off to a bad start, was racing downhill out of control.

The front office bell ding-donged again. Was it always so busy on a Monday afternoon?

"I'd like to adopt Honey," I blurted out. With so many visitors, I couldn't risk someone else adopting her if I dilly-dallied around.

Jane's fingers tightened in Honey's soft fur in a proprietary way.

"Oh? I'll have to do a home visit, and there's an application you need to fill out," she replied. Then her eyes narrowed, and she asked, "Didn't you just arrive in Frog Hollow today?"

I wondered how the heck she knew that little detail. Worse than that, though, was her scowl that suggested she'd pegged me as unsuitable and unreliable in the adoptee department.

"That's true, but Frog Hollow is my home now. My grandmother, Audrey Fernsby, left Moonlight Mansion to me."

"I know. Everyone knows about that, but you'll still need references."

Jane turned and opened the door, holding it and gesturing for me to go inside. As I passed Honey, sitting quietly next to Jane the whole time we spoke, she snatched the leash from my hand. With a loud click, she snapped it on Honey's collar.

I saw a flash of gauzy white in the walkway ahead that disappeared as soon as I blinked. It was comforting, though, to know Audrey watched over me even if I had no idea what she was actually doing or how she could help.

"Where *is* Will?" Jane muttered from behind me. "It's not usually so busy on a Monday. If he left early, I'll..."

She left her thought unfinished, and, to be honest, I really didn't want to know what she'd do to him because I was sure she was capable of just about anything.

I stopped and waited for Jane to lead the way to wherever we were going. She stopped at Honey's kennel and pushed the door open for her to enter, but Honey balked. She strained backward against the leash. A loud shriek pierced the quiet space. I jumped. Then, with both hands cradling her face, Jane slumped against the bars. Honey, dragging the leash, moved behind me with her tail between her legs.

Without thinking, I peered around Jane to see what the problem was. A cold breeze swirled around me, causing goosebumps to prickle the skin on my arms.

The iron smell of blood assaulted my nose, overpowering the underlying antiseptic aroma. There, in the back corner of the kennel, I saw a horrifying vision. Clive, slumped over, his hand, covered with blood and clutching the handle of a knife stuck in his shoulder. I think he'd tried to pull it out because there was blood everywhere, oozing around the blade and soaking his shirt. Light reflected from the handle, turning Audrey's Tattoo Guy a sickening bluish-gray color.

"Is he dead?" I mumbled, hoping Jane had a clue.

He groaned, startling me. I moved back with no intention of going near him and stepped on something hard. I looked down and saw a few colorful gemstones at my feet. Without thinking, I grabbed them and stuffed them in my pocket. Then, I picked up Honey's leash and shook Jane out of her paralyzing shocked state.

"Do something! This is your shelter, your employee. Help him!" I shouted at her.

"Find Will," she said before taking tentative steps into the kennel.

I didn't wait to see what she did next. Instead, I ran outside with Honey. The bright sunshine shocked me after the gloom of the shelter, blinding me for a moment. If I didn't know better, this seemed like a normal day with birds chirping and mosquitoes buzzing around my face. But of course, today was anything but normal.

I scanned the parking lot and spotted two cars and a truck—my red BMW, the old Volvo I'd seen Jane drive off in, and the beat-up truck—parked side by side. No sign of the motorcycle I'd seen earlier.

"Will's gone. I saw him run away from Honey's kennel, then I heard a motorcycle roar off," Audrey whispered even though we were outside and away from Jane.

"You think he stabbed Tattoo Guy?" I asked, horrified that an assault actually happened only a doorway away from where I'd been standing. I also couldn't wrap my head around that Will, who'd seemed so friendly and nice, might be the perpetrator. Unthinkable!

"I don't know," Audrey said, sounding unhappy with her admission. "I should have watched Tattoo Guy like a hawk, but I wanted to check on you, too. Either someone came into the shelter, or Will, who was the only other person here, had enough of Tattoo Guy's insolence, and..." she made a sound like a death gurgle.

"Jane returned while I was out back with Honey," I said, remembering the last ten or fifteen minutes. "You warned me that she was coming, remember?"

Audrey floated around the parking lot. Moving around was a familiar behavior she'd always displayed when nervous or thinking or planning something. In this instance, it was probably all three.

"True. I took my eyes off Jane to warn you since she was on her way looking madder than a wet cat. How was I supposed to know someone would try to kill Tattoo Guy in that short time?"

"Don't beat yourself up, Audrey. None of that matters

right now. Tattoo Guy is lying in a pool of blood with me right here in the middle of another mess. I'm sure Officer Brooksby will have my head when he finds me here. I'm going in to check on Jane; see if she called the police yet."

I wasn't looking forward to another interrogation from Brooksby, but if he was on his way, I planned to account for every second I'd been at the shelter. Finding me here at the location of a second crime scene? He'd probably thank his lucky stars he could wrap up the mystery quickly and lock me away without blinking.

That thought did *not* work for me in any shape or form.

When I turned around to go back inside to check on Jane, she was standing in the doorway, her brows scrunched together. "Who were you talking to?"

Honey barked and wagged her plummy tail. I patted her and tried to quickly come up with a reasonable explanation.

Jane walked toward me, now with a grin spread across her face. "Oh, you're comforting Honey. She had a terrible shock, didn't she? I know most people think I'm a little kooky because I talk to the dogs, but you know what? I really don't care what they think. And what I'm thinking now is that maybe you aren't so bad after all."

Was that a compliment? Maybe in an inside-out kind of way. She took my arm and pulled me back inside to the office.

Phew. I'd just dodged a dicey situation when Jane assumed I was talking to Honey. Of course, who would guess in a million decades that it was actually a ghost who had my attention? I wiped the film of sweat off my brow and thanked my lucky stars or whatever had intervened.

"Jane, that was a terrible shock. Have you recovered?"

From the way she stared at me, you'd think I'd just asked

her to shut down her shelter. "No one recovers from something like that. The image is forever seared on my brain. And the smell?" A tremor surged through her body. "After you went outside, I checked Clive, put pressure on the bleeding until it stopped, and got him comfortable on a pile of blankets. I promised I'd be right back, but who knows if that even registered."

I said, "You'll have to talk to the police. You did call them, didn't you?" I was relieved that Clive was still alive. If he pulled through, he might be able to provide the police with some answers to lead us to the murderer, assuming whoever attacked Clive also killed Vernon.

Jane nodded and settled onto her creaky chair. Honey sat next to her, whining for attention and pawing at Jane's leg. The poor thing must be thoroughly confused.

"Jane? You asked me to find Will, but I didn't see him or his motorcycle. Are you sure you didn't pass him or anyone else when you drove back from talking to Officer Brooksby?"

"To be honest? I'm not sure. I was thinking about Prince Dasher and Vernon and you. But, no, I don't remember seeing anyone. I think..." she stood up, walked around her desk, and tossed Honey's leash to me.

"Here. Take Honey and leave. Right now. I can't return her to that kennel with Clive, and I don't have time to get her adjusted to sharing with another dog. I'll tell Officer Brooksby that when I returned no one was here, and I found Clive bleeding in the kennel. Okay?"

I couldn't believe what I was hearing, and a nagging voice, maybe Audrey's, warned me that this was a terrible idea. I ignored the warning, though, and took the leash, thinking only of helping Honey.

Jane heaped my arms with a dark blue blanket, a food

bowl, and a small bag of food. "I'll be in touch as soon as possible," she said.

What the heck was I getting involved in?

## 14

Honey happily jumped onto the back seat of my car. I, on the other hand, hesitated. After furtively glancing around, checking for witnesses to my escape from the scene of a crime, I decided the coast was clear and slid in behind the wheel.

"Just get going, Nikki," Audrey hissed. "The longer you dawdle, the more chance someone will actually see you here."

Her voice came at me from the empty passenger seat, which I guess wasn't actually empty. If you can call a ghost a passenger.

"If Jane convinces Brooksby no one else was at the shelter, you dodged a bullet. And, for goodness sake, take the back way out. Otherwise, you'll risk passing the police."

Audrey was right. I'd forgotten that the route leading to the Underdog Animal Shelter turned into a little-used dirt road that would bring us back to Hoppin' John Highway, well away from the police department's prying eyes. I wasn't free and clear yet, but all this activity had pumped up my adrenaline.

I sped off, quickly hitting the unpaved section of the road, which had my fancy car flying over bumps and ruts and adding more scratches to the side from all the branches that desperately needed a trim. In addition, the wind blew my hair around my face, and streaks and shadows flickered like strobe lights in this canopied tunnel.

"I think you're enjoying this," Audrey said. "Am I wrong, or has playing detective settled in?"

I cast a side-eye to the seemingly vacant passenger seat. "It's definitely a rush," I admitted, "but I could do without the murder. And the attempted murder happened way too close," I added.

Audrey chuckled.

Blood and gore had always made me squeamish, but obviously, that came with murder. Once I got used to it, this detecting stuff could make a living in Frog Hollow interesting, assuming there were more murders. Ghoulish thought, but who knew what the future might bring?

"Let's figure out what we know," Audrey said, now a shimmery white transparency next to me. "You and Will were at the shelter when Clive was attacked. Will told you he saw Vernon talking to Clive before he adopted Dash, so that could be an important connection."

"And Vernon is dead, and Clive is clinging to life."

"Which leaves Will."

I slowed down and looked at Audrey. "You think Will did this to both of them?"

"Well, think about it," she said in her wise grandmotherly voice. "He loves the animals. Dash told you that Clive wasn't very nice. Vernon adopted Dash under what sounds like suspicious circumstances. Will decided to get rid of the bad guys for the sake of the animals, then he jumped ship. What else can it all add up to?"

Sirens wailed in the distance, so I pulled over to wait it out. No sense ending up on Hoppin' John Highway right in the middle of that chaos.

I considered Audrey's theory, but I couldn't see Will as a murderer. Sure, he was invested in the animals, but a killer? There had to be other ways to protect the dogs and cats.

"You forgot about Jane," I said. "As far as we know, Clive was fine when she returned to the shelter. Maybe she's a great actress and faked her shock."

"But she let you leave, Niks. Wouldn't it make more sense for her to point the finger at you instead of..."

"Oh, no!"

We both turned at the exact same moment and stared at each other with our mouths wide open. I slammed my hands on the steering wheel. Honey put her head on my shoulder and whimpered.

"Sorry, girl. You don't like loud noises, do you?" I caressed her soft fur while the reality of my action settled in like a big dark storm cloud.

Why, oh why did I ignore the nagging voice that clearly told me it was a bad idea to take Honey and leave? Of course, hindsight is always clear as a summer day without a cloud in the sky. It would have been far better to have stayed and faced the music with Officer Brooksby instead of letting a bit of fear, and an easy out send me running like a bunny from the jaws of a rabid fox.

Yes, I did have another motive, I reminded myself. Saving Honey from more anxiety. Okay, that was an exaggeration, but I realized I'd made a terrible blunder. Now, Jane could plant something to connect me to Clive's attack. Did I leave anything behind? Maybe a granola bar wrapper fell out of my pocket? Definitely fingerprints.

"I walked right into Jane's devious plan, didn't I? She'll

have plenty of time to clean up any evidence that points to her and plant something that leads the police right to me. She saw me arrive and could tell the police that it was me who attacked Clive, stole Honey, then disappeared."

"When you put it that way, Niks," Audrey mumbled, "it sounds pretty bad. The good news is *we* know you didn't kill Vernon or attack Clive, so all we have to do is find the real criminal. Easy peasy, right?"

At the moment, Audrey's spin on this horrible situation sounded the tiniest bit above pathetic, but it did cut to the only solution. I tapped my fingers on the steering wheel, waiting for the sirens to move beyond our escape route.

"Tick-tock," I said impatiently to the rearview mirror.

I changed the subject and turned to Audrey's ephemeral presence next to me. "First, we have to find Will," I said. "He might have something on Jane to help us nail her before…"

"But what if he's the bad guy, Niks? We don't know for sure that Jane's the perp."

Perp? I thought. She's really getting into this detective speak.

"I don't know," I said. "I'll cross that bridge… or jump off it when the time comes. Now? I don't hear the sirens anymore, so I'm high-tailing it back to Moonlight Mansion. Maybe Dash has some ideas about all this."

I wasn't convinced he was a reliable witness to anything, but he was all I had to work with for now. I drove to the end of Leafy Lane and turned onto Hoppin' John Highway, which left us a few short miles to get back to Live Oak Lane and home.

"Niks?" Audrey mused. "If Dash is somehow connected to both murders, how will you keep him safe?"

Good question and I had no answer. But I was confident

I'd keep the dachshund safe because the alternative wasn't an option.

"He'll be fine," I said. "Like you told me earlier, having a talking dog will be very helpful, and I can see all kinds of possibilities even if I can't foresee the future."

"Yee-haw, Niks!" Audrey screeched like the cowgirl she'd always dreamed of being. "You'll succeed because you have to."

I wish I felt that confident.

"We've got our first detective case, Niks, and it's a doozy. Nothing like jumping in with both feet and everything else to learn how to solve a crime."

When our eyes met, hers glowed the deepest, purest blue I'd ever seen. I chalked it up to extreme excitement.

But I rolled my eyes until it made me dizzy.

Yeah, nothing like jumping in blind. Audrey could screech all she wanted. I, on the other hand, needed to keep a level head and my eyes on the clues.

Clues!

I glanced into the back seat where I'd dumped everything Jane had given me for Honey.

"Audrey? Something just occurred to me."

"Can't wait to hear it." She rubbed her ghostly hands together with glee.

"Vernon was covered with a dark blue blanket, right?"

She nodded.

"Dash said he smelled cats and insisted cats had killed Vernon. That's totally ridiculous, but what does make sense..." I refilled my lungs, "is that the blanket smelled like cats because it probably came from the shelter. I spotted a big pile of dark blue blankets in the office."

"Bingo!" Audrey said, and if I felt reckless, I'd have taken my eyes off the road and seen Audrey pretending to aim a pair of six-shooters. "And there's the connection you need, Niks. Brilliant sleuthing. The killer got the blanket from the shelter, killed Vernon, and returned to the shelter to kill Clive. Only problem is, Clive is still alive, and hopefully, soon, he'll be able to shed light on this mess."

"It's a connection, but who's the killer? It has to be someone who had access to the shelter." That seemed to be the one factor common to both victims.

"Will or Jane," she said.

While I drove on autopilot, my brain worked at warp speed. "Those two, yes, but other people looking to adopt must have been at the shelter, too. What about someone who recently adopted a cat or dog? Does Jane give everyone a blue blanket to take home with their new furbaby?"

The dark blue blanket stuck out like a road sign, but what exactly did it mean? I mumbled as if I'd been alone, trying to piece this puzzle together.

"If the blanket covering Vernon belonged to Dash, the killer must have taken it out of his car. And that explains why Birdie didn't find a blanket in the stuff she grabbed from the trunk. Something doesn't add up. Is this all about that bag of gemstones Birdie found?"

Too many questions, and not enough answers.

By now, we'd arrived home, my sanctuary if there was such a thing in my current topsy-turvy, drama-filled life. Unfortunately, an unwelcome surprise waited, in the shape of a rusty car parked under the shade of a big oak tree.

"What's Lacey doing here?" I asked, not that I expected Audrey to have a clue.

She waved her arm through the air, sending a cold breeze that rustled the loose tendrils that escaped my messy bun, and I pushed them back from my face.

"It's her day to do Birdie's hair," she answered, like, duh, you should know this fact. I guess the blank expression on my face made Audrey explain further.

"Birdie's red hair doesn't happen without a lot of help, you know. Lacey comes every Monday at three o'clock. On the dot."

Of course, I knew about Birdie's hair obsession, even though Birdie insisted it was her natural, God-given hair color. We'd long pretended to believe that lie. But one part of that explanation caught like a bad case of the shingles. I suddenly realized that Lacey May Dawson would be in *my* house right now when I needed peace and quiet to think through everything that had happened concerning Dash, Vernon, and Clive.

"Don't get all pouty, Niks," Audrey said. I could never keep my emotions hidden from her. "Lacey has changed. Plus, as the town hairdresser, she knows everyone in Frog Hollow. Think about that because she could be a handy bit of help. Please turn on your charm and shove that silly old competition stuff you had with her far away, okay?"

"Okay," I said, but I wasn't sure I could forget how she had always, always gone after every boy I'd ever shown a tiny bit of interest in. I'd never be able to trust her as far as I could throw her.

And, throwing her out of my house sounded pretty darn tempting right about now. I put on my game-face and walked inside with Honey tugging at the leash by my side.

Dash's nails tap-tapped on the floor of the vestibule as he did his short-legged dance around me, whining and wagging his tail like it had a mind of its own.

"I missed you, Nikki. Missed you, missed you, missed you!" he said in a rising crescendo. He acted like I'd been gone for years on a trip around the world.

I crouched down and scooped him into my arms. "I've

only been gone for an hour, two at the most, Dash. Everything okay here?"

He lapped my chin until my only choice was to put him down. Then he saw Honey and went completely bonkers.

"Honey!" he shrieked along with a loud howl. "My love! I missed you!"

His love? How did he fall in love with her in the first place? The plus side was that I didn't have to worry about him being jealous of another dog in the mansion.

The two dogs proceeded to wag their tails and sniff each other's butts while I stood to one side like I'd been reduced to chopped liver now that Honey had Dash's attention. I hated to admit that I wasn't thrilled with this new pecking order.

Audrey breezed past me with what had become a familiar blast of cool air. "Hurry along, Niks," she whispered breathlessly. "If you're lucky, Lacey will fix up your hair, too."

Over my dead body, I thought.

## 15

"Come on, Nikki," Dash said as he followed behind Audrey's invisible trail. Honey followed, too, staying glued to his side. The poor girl. At least she seemed comfortable with her four-legged admirer.

"Dash?"

He stopped, turned his head, and looked up at me with a less than adoring expression. I hoped it would wear off once he got used to having Honey in the house. "Yes, Nikki?"

I was a little put off by his formal politeness. From him, it sounded a bit condescending. "What's going on here, Dash?"

"You must be referring to Lacey, aren't you? I love her. She brought delicious cookies for me. Now, come on!"

This development made the hairs on my neck stand up, and my toes curl. How did she even know he was here? Right, she must have seen him in my car earlier, and now Lacey Dawson had Dash in the palm of her hand. Where did that leave me? She had to have an ulterior motive, and I didn't like it.

With all the craziness happening around me, suspicious

was my new second nature. Better to be suspicious and careful than cavalier and dead, I told myself.

I walked into Birdie's spacious kitchen, where Lacey had her portable hairdressing chair set up in an alcove. Light poured in through the window and turned Birdie's locks into a glistening red halo. I had to blink several times before my eyes adjusted to the brightness.

Lacey held bits of hair between her two fingers and snipped. She squirted some gel into the palm of her hand and worked it into Birdie's hair, creating an unholy mess as far as I was concerned. Then she puffed the back and sides with her hands, picked up a mirror, and handed it to Birdie.

"What do you think?" she asked.

Birdie tilted the mirror and her head one way and then the other, her eyes lighting up when she saw me in the reflection.

"Nikki? Don't just stand there like a signpost. Say hello to Lacey."

"Hi," I said but without a shred of enthusiasm.

Lacey turned around and smiled a big, bright, I'm-thrilled-to-see-you-again grin that filled her whole face. I wasn't buying it.

"Hi, again, Nikki. I had a cancellation, so I can stay and squeeze you in for a quick trim if you'd like."

Did I hear a smirk in her tone or was it my suspicious imagination kicking in. I had no idea what to think anymore.

Birdie swiveled the chair around so she faced me. Her new cut framed her face with the sides curling to her chin. The back barely touched her collar, and the spikes on top? I had no idea what I could say about that look. The combination of fire engine red and spikes made it look like she'd stuck her finger in a socket. At least as far as I was concerned.

"It's, um... amazing," I finally managed to blurt out, which thankfully was a totally honest observation. With any luck, Birdie would take it as a compliment. Otherwise, my diet for the foreseeable future would consist of peanut butter and jelly sandwiches.

"I know. Lacey's a genius with hair," Birdie gushed. The broad smile told me that she loved this new look, and apparently, my comment passed scrutiny. I breathed a sigh of relief.

Dash jumped onto Birdie's lap and sniffed the new hairdo. "Not my style, but it works on her. If you ever spike my hair, I'll gnaw your toes off," he said before he jumped back down to stand next to Honey.

I wiggled my toes. Dash had nothing to worry about, so my toes were safe.

"Oh, my goodness!" Lacey exclaimed. She knelt on the floor and wrapped her arms around Honey's neck. "It's so good to see you out of the kennel. Are you living here with Nikki? What a lucky, lucky girl."

Dash's tail started up again, and he gave Lacey a lick for good measure. Apparently, anyone who liked Honey was a friend of Dash's. The cookies she brought hadn't hurt her standing either, pitting me against some tough competition.

Lacey stood up and tossed her scissors on the kitchen island. They landed with a loud clang. With a professional flourish, she unfastened the gown draped around Birdie and shook off the loose hair.

"There you go, darlin'. Same time next week?"

"Of course," Birdie said and dug in her purse for money, handing a wad to Lacey. "I added extra. Nikki's cut is on me." She gave me her don't-even-think-about-arguing glare.

Lacey held her hand out toward the empty chair. "Well?" Her tilted head and one raised eyebrow felt like a dare.

I wasn't sure if the dare was about defying Birdie or submitting to Lacey's scissors. The second choice was far safer.

I sat. I absolutely didn't want spikes in my hair, but now I was committed. Lacey swiveled the chair to face the window, fluffed the gown, and let it fall around me. With a quick movement, she fastened it tightly around my neck. I fought the urge to choke. Then, she tenderly ran her fingers through my thick locks.

"Such beautiful hair, Nikki. Maybe just a trim?"

"That would be perfect," I answered and relaxed into the cushy seat now that I knew her plan.

After a heavy spritzing over my hair, Lacey dragged a comb through it, lightly pulling on the tangles. I was impressed.

"How in the world did you get Jane to let Honey go home with you? Will told me she always does a home visit first." Lacey held her scissors up and clicked them open and shut.

"Well..." I stared at the sharp scissors wondering how much information I should share.

"Just tell them," Audrey mumbled from somewhere close to my ear. "You can trust Lacey."

"You can't bring Honey back to that awful place!" Dash screeched from behind me.

I was bombarded on both sides by a ghost and dog. I closed my eyes and blocked them out, preparing myself to focus on rhythmic tugs and snips instead of the verbal assault.

"There was an incident at the shelter," I said.

"You call what happened an incident?" Audrey huffed

and sent a breeze that ruffled my hair. If she wasn't careful, Lacey might discover her ghostly afterlife.

"Is there a window open?" Lacey asked.

Birdie made a show of cranking the windows closed even though neither one in front of me was even cracked an inch.

"An incident?" she asked after she turned around and stood in front of me with her arms crossed. "What kind of incident, Nikki?"

"Well, remember the guy you told me about who works at the shelter? His name is Clive," I said. "He has a lot of tattoos," I added for Birdie and Lacey's benefit.

"Ouch! Dang, scissors are razor sharp. I cut myself when you said that son-of-a-slug's name." Lacey sucked the tip of her finger, and I carefully slid away from the hand that still held her scissors. I didn't want to be the next accident waiting to happen.

"That guy is slug slime," she added as if she hadn't already made her contempt for Clive crystal clear.

I snorted after that description and slid completely out of the chair. It seemed safer to move away from her and her scissors until she'd calmed down. On a positive note, though, Lacey moved up a notch from the bottom of the people-I-knew-in-Frog-Hollow list since we had someone in common that we both found repulsive.

"Let's take a little break, and I'll make tea," Birdie said to my relief. She didn't wait for any replies but moved to the sink, filled the tea kettle, and put it on the burner.

"Do you have time, Lacey? Just a quick break while Nikki tells us what happened at the shelter."

I had no argument with that plan.

"And cookies?" Dash said. "Honey's hungry."

I laughed and gave both dogs a good pat. "You'd like a treat, Honey? Dash already had his, but you can have one."

"No fair! No fair!" he yelped as he jumped up and down. He barely even reached Honey's chin.

Dash's desperate attempt to outsmart me in order to get a treat was funny, but I tried not to laugh for too long. I handed both dogs one of the cookies Lacey had brought for Dash.

"Not funny, Nikki."

My stomach rumbled, reminding me that I'd only eaten a granola bar since breakfast. I was about to rummage through the cupboards for snacks, but Birdie was way ahead of me. She set a plate with slices of her delicious apple bread on the island along with the teapot, cups, and honey.

"Grab a stool and help yourselves," she said. Birdie also tossed a waterproof bandage to Lacey. "Now, Nikki, tell us all about the incident at the shelter."

Lacey nursed her finger and sat down. She didn't waste a second helping herself to Birdie's goodies, and I didn't either.

After inhaling one piece of the sweet bread, I said, "Someone tried to kill Clive."

"Tried to?" Lacey said with one eyebrow raised. "But failed to succeed? That's too bad."

I sipped the tea—peach and sweetened just the way I loved it. "He was bleeding and groaning when I left but no, not dead."

"Who did it?" Lacey asked between bites, never taking her eyes off me.

"I don't know. Besides me, Will and Jane were the only people that I know for certain were there. I was in the play yard with Honey when the front bell rang, so someone must have come in. Will left to check, but I never saw anyone else.

Lacey leaned on the table, her eyes wide with emotion—concern, suspense, excitement—which one, I wasn't sure. "What exactly happened to Clive?"

"Someone stabbed him."

"Was it you?" she asked with awe lacing her tone.

"No!"

"Then maybe it was Will or Jane," Lacey said matter-of-factly and took another piece of apple bread. She held the bread half-way to her mouth but stopped and stared off into space like something important had just occurred to her. Happily, this conversation had pushed any thoughts about cutting my hair to a faraway place on her to-do list. Fine with me.

"Exactly what I thought," I said because who else could it be? "How well do you know them?" I asked.

"Well," Lacey said, giving Birdie and me pointed stares. "Will can't stand Clive. He told me that Clive sometimes hits the dogs to let them know who's boss. I could never figure out why Jane kept him around except for the rumors." Again, Lacey looked at us like we were co-conspirators.

"Rumors? About what?" I asked.

Birdie and I, captivated by Lacey's breathless narration, leaned into Lacey.

"Jane suspected that Clive was involved in something illegal. Some scheme she was determined to figure out. Maybe she kept him around to keep an eye on him."

"How do you know this," I asked.

She shrugged. "People talk when they're getting their hair cut. Jane comes in for a trim once in a while. But, there's more." Lacey paused to finish the apple bread. "Clive hit Honey, and then Dash bit him. They were kennel mates, you know. For the short time Dash was there." Lacey sat back in her chair, her voice returning to normal. "I don't know.

Maybe Jane had had enough and stabbed him. I heard Clive was related to her, but I don't know anyone who actually liked that slug."

I almost spilled my tea. "Dash bit Clive?" I shot a look in his direction. "Good boy! That explains his connection to Honey. He's her short-legged knight in furry armor."

Dash barked and barked. "I did! I did! He tasted awful. Like a possum. He looks like a possum too, with beady eyes and pointy ears."

I looked at Birdie and shrugged. She probably suspected that Dash told me something, but I couldn't tell her with Lacey sitting with us.

"So, Nikki," Lacey said, looking smug and very comfortable at the table with Birdie and me. "Are you going to investigate?"

I sprayed a mouthful of tea across the island. "Me? Investigate?"

"Yeah. Birdie told me you're starting a detective agency." Her eyes lit up like two sparklers. "Can I help?"

Audrey hovered behind Lacey, twisting one way and then the other in an over-the-top and obvious, to me at least, attempt to get my attention. But I'll admit, Audrey was hard to ignore. When I finally gave her the attention she craved, she nodded vigorously and gave me two thumbs up. Apparently, my grandmother voted to let Lacey Dawson help investigate the odd happenings here in Frog Hollow.

How long had I been back here at Moonlight Mansion? Surely not long enough for so many plots to crash land in my lap.

But here I was, still on day one in this crazy, mixed-up new world with another important decision to make.

## 16

I looked at Lacey, really studying her. She had a fierce determination etched on her face below her poufy bleached blonde pile of hair. I tried my hardest to keep an open mind about her offer, but her look reminded me of something I couldn't quite put my finger on.

The stubborn clench in Lacey's jaw and her over-the-top make-up and hairstyle reminded me of a pit bull mixed with a poodle. Did that make her a Pitdle or a Pitpoo? Pitpoo sounded best.

"What's so funny?" Dash asked.

Apparently, I'd laughed out loud, and now my little crew consisting of Birdie, Dash, Audrey, and yes, even Lacey stared at me like I'd lost my mind. Probably somewhere between the two murder victims, I suppose. Another giggle erupted from my chest.

With a herculean effort, I wiped what I assumed was a silly grin off my face and said, "Lacey, you can help under one condition."

"Sure," she said without an ounce of hesitation. With

her pinky, she dabbed crumbs off the edge of her lips and waited politely for me to utter my demand.

Birdie, with one eyebrow raised in an I-can't-wait-to-hear-what's next slant, said nothing, but her silence always unnerved me to a certain degree. She knew me so well I was positive she'd already guessed what had come between my friendship with Lacey more than ten years earlier.

I took a deep breath. It was now or never to get this out of my system. The new me wasn't going to worry about someone else's feelings over my own. I didn't mean that in a rude way, of course, but I had to be true to myself. Life was too short for dancing around a bush filled with nonsense. Right?

"Lacey," I said with the assurance I felt deep within myself, "you have to promise to be honest with me all the time. And no interfering in any way whatsoever if I find a special someone."

Lacey stared at me as if I'd just landed from Mars.

"When we were teenagers," I said, "you always tried to steal every guy I even looked at twice during my summer vacations here."

I should have said that over ten years ago, but no, I never straightened things out. I'd let it simmer and bug me since we were eighteen. Fourteen years was long enough. I felt lighter already.

Lacey stared at me. "I wasn't interested in those goofy boys."

"You weren't? Why'd you do it then?" This didn't add up to what I'd always imagined.

"I was interested in you, silly." Then she laughed so hard I wondered if she'd peed herself. Birdie joined the hysteria. I couldn't see Audrey, but I imagined she left for fear of being unable to control herself after hearing that declaration.

Me? If the heat factor in my face meant anything, I had to be several shades darker than Birdie's new red hairdo. My smug expression vanished, and I felt like I'd inhaled a rotten peach.

"Oh, my goodness, Nikki," Lacey said between hiccups of laughter. "I wasn't interested in you the way you're thinking." Lots more laughter interrupted her words, but for the life of me, I didn't see anything funny in this new development.

"I wanted to be your best friend," she finally managed to explain. "If you had a boyfriend hanging around all the time, I figured you wouldn't have a second to spare for a girlfriend. You never knew that?" She looked genuinely hurt now.

"For these past fourteen years, while you acted like I was worse than doo on your sneaker, you thought I wanted to steal those boys away from you? Heck, Nikki, you should thank me. I did you a favor. Not one of those losers deserved you."

Lacey had deep feelings, and she couldn't hide them if she wanted to. Profound sadness replaced her laughing face from a moment ago.

She was right about those boys, but I'd only figured it out years later. One after another of those *popular* boys ended up in jail or on drugs or who knows what other disaster they managed to make of their lives. Lacey really did save me from a lot of heartache. And I'd shown her nothing but a big cold shoulder.

I stared at her. What on earth should I say now? Should I apologize? Wrap her in a bear hug? Tell her that I was an idiot all those years ago?

Birdie stopped laughing and wiped the corners of her eyes before she came to my rescue with a safer subject.

"Lacey has to get back to her salon, but I invited her to come back for breakfast tomorrow morning. We can discuss how to proceed with the investigation in more detail then."

"Breakfast?" Dash said, pawing at my leg. "I need food now," he whined like a spoiled two-year-old.

"No begging, Dash," I said and scooped him onto my lap. "You'll get your dinner at five o'clock. That's the routine."

"I can't wait!" he moaned and crumpled into a shivering heap like he was in the throes of a near-death event.

I put him on the floor. "First, we're going outside for a walk. You and Honey need to learn the boundaries. It's important you stay near the house."

Lacey interrupted my conversation, reminding me that I needed to be more careful with my Dash conversations.

"How cute! I love how you talk to little Dash. I bet he understands what you're saying, too."

Birdie stacked the teacups and brought them to the sink, then turned to face Lacey. "You can't imagine," she said. "That dog is smarter than a wily coyote. Especially when it comes to food. If I didn't know better, it's almost like he chose Nikki to be his one and only. Right, Nikki?"

She winked at me from behind Lacey's back.

"Almost." I stood up. "Let's go, you two. See you back here tomorrow, Lacey."

I opened the kitchen door and walked outside before I said anything else in front of her that might be a little too strange. The last thing I needed right now was anyone getting suspicious about my secret ability to talk to Dash. Mostly because it was just too hard to explain. But then again, who would even believe it?

"I like her," Dash said once we were outside with the door closed firmly behind us. "She'll make a good friend."

Maybe, but I wasn't going to make any rash decision about that. She acted like she'd changed, and both Audrey and Birdie seemed to like her. But... how did I know she didn't have an ulterior motive?

We walked toward Audrey's koi pond. The water, and especially the fountain captured Dash's attention. He stared with a fascination that seemed odd, but at least it distracted him from Lacey.

"What's swimming in there?"

"Fish."

"Can I eat them?"

"No! Those koi are special to Audrey, and she'd never forgive you. You don't want to incur the wrath of a ghost," I said, trying to sound as stern as possible.

He leaned over the pond with his nose almost touching the water lilies. Before I could stop him, he snapped at the water. "I almost caught it," he shouted with glee.

I pulled him away from the pond before he managed to catch himself a snack. "Now listen carefully, Dash. Those fish are not a snack for you. Look over there." I pointed to the edge of the grass. "See that stone wall? Don't go beyond that boundary, and keep Honey on this side, too. There's plenty of lawn and bushes for sniffing and playing, but don't go into the woods."

He looked at me. I could see him cooking up a scheme behind those dark brown intelligent eyes, and I didn't like it.

I knelt down and balanced on my knees in front of him. "Dash, do you understand? This is important. I'm afraid someone might try to steal you."

He dropped his head. Even his long ears sagged. "I understand," he said in a pathetic voice. "But who would want to steal *me*? My own family kicked me out." He sounded so sad I dug into my pocket for a treat and tossed it to him. Was I being overly suspicious? Probably.

But I knew something dangerous was going on. Whether Dash knew it or not, he was involved. Which meant I was too.

## 17

Fortunately, Dash had the attention span of a two-year-old, especially if Honey was around. He trotted over to a section of the garden where Honey sniffed around some particularly thick foliage. She seemed to have found something interesting under the boxwood hedge. Perfect. Thank you, Honey, I said silently. I could use a moment or two to myself.

Dash pushed in front of his girlfriend. His attraction to her gave me a break from his neediness now and then. Satisfied that he was safely occupied, I sighed but didn't take my eyes off the pair.

"Psst!"

Fear sizzled up my spine, and cold fingers squeezed my heart. Today I was alert to every possible threat. Every hair stood up like a chill had suddenly blown past me, especially when I knew it definitely wasn't an Audrey-style breeze.

"Nikki. I need to talk to you. Walk toward the stone wall. I'm standing behind the big twisted cedar tree."

I recognized the voice and scanned the area but saw no one. "Will? What are you doing here?"

Dash and Honey, busy with their own investigation, hadn't noticed the intruder. Was Audrey around somewhere keeping an eye on me? I had no idea. The only consolation was that I didn't think Will would have warned me of his presence if he meant to do me harm, right?

As a precaution, I picked up one of the rocks that bordered the koi pond. The smooth weight fit in my palm, providing a degree of security that boosted my confidence. So, I walked to the edge of the lawn, and to give myself cover, I bent down and admired the tulips. I loved their bright, bold colors as much as I admired the heady aroma of the lilacs blooming near the dogs frolicking like reunited best friends do. I hoped I looked natural.

"What are you doing here?" I hissed, not exactly sure where Will lurked or why he was here.

"You and Dash have really bonded," he whispered back. I heard admiration in his voice. "That's good. And, I'm glad you have Honey, but how did you get her here so quickly? It usually takes a home visit and tons of paperwork before Jane lets a dog leave the shelter."

I ignored his question. That wasn't important right now or even any of his business. At least not until I knew why he'd disappeared into thin air after Clive's assault.

"Why are you here, Will?"

"I need help," he answered like I should have figured that out myself.

I glanced at the dogs. Dash had his nose in the air. Had he caught Will's scent? I turned my attention back to my uninvited guest.

"Why? Because you tried to kill Clive and need an alibi? Forget it!" I saw no point in beating around the bush on that topic.

Will stepped partway out from behind the tree. Worry,

exhaustion, and dirt marred his handsome face. His light brown hair, looking as if he'd just tumbled out of bed, might have fooled someone else, but the bits of leaves stuck here and there reminded me that he was a man on the run.

"Clive isn't dead?"

I heard a note of surprise and possibly relief.

"He wasn't when I left. Will, did you kill Vernon and try to kill Clive?" As I stared into his dark, unreadable eyes waiting for his answer, I hoped with all my being I wasn't staring into the eyes of a murderer.

"Nikki, I swear." He wiped his brow and looked over his shoulder. "I wasn't anywhere near Vernon, but I understand why you think I attacked Clive. The front bell rang and I left you and Honey outside, remember?"

He looked at me hopefully. I nodded.

"Well," he said, carefully. "I saw Clive slumped in Honey's kennel. I probably should have tried to help him but I focused on catching the person responsible. So, I ran to the office, then outside, hoping to find who had attacked him. Clive was far from my favorite person, but I never wished him harm." He ran his fingers through his hair, dislodging some of the debris. "Do you believe me?"

Did I? He stared at me like my answer was the most important thing in the world to him.

"Did you see anyone?" I asked, sidestepping his question.

He shook his head. "I jumped on my motorcycle and raced off, hoping to catch up to someone. Dumb probably, but that's what happened."

"Did you ever catch up to a car?"

"No." He let out a deep frustrated sigh. "Nothing. But I took the dirt road, thinking that's what I'd do if I'd just committed a crime. Maybe the attacker went the other way.

Now, since I fled like that, I'm sure I look guilty of something."

I didn't disagree.

Honey flew past me, leaped over the stone wall, and barreled straight to Will with Dash close behind. Although, with his much shorter legs, his charge was not particularly elegant.

"Nikki, Nice Guy always has treats," Dash said without stopping until he was sitting next to Honey.

As Will gave them cuddles like he hadn't seen them for years, I heard the sound of a car door slam, an engine roar to life, and tires crunch on the way out of the driveway. Lacey, I supposed.

Will busily dug in his pockets and handed a treat to each dog. "I don't believe it spoils them. Not when they've lived at a shelter and have so little to look forward to. I know, I know, they're out now, but I can't break this habit," he said guiltily.

"You don't have to make excuses to me, Will. I'll probably do the same."

Dash looked at me. "I heard that, Nikki. You said treats whenever I want, right?"

"I need to get some tiny treats, so Dash won't put on weight," I said.

Will chuckled.

Before Dash had a chance to sputter an objection, I heard the crunching sound again coming up the driveway. Did Lacey forget something?

Will's attention went beyond me, to the house. He stared and scowled. "Did a car just drive in?"

"Lacey was here, but she just left."

"No, not that car. A different car just drove in." He crouched down and crab walked to his hiding spot behind the tree. The dogs joined, maybe thinking this was a new game, but I'd seen the panicked look on Will's face.

He made himself as small as possible. "It's my grandfather. There's no mistaking the sound of his oversized engine. Listen, I'm not ready to talk to him yet. I have to leave, and I'm taking Honey. If he asks about her, tell him she ran off."

"Why would your grandfather ask about Honey?" All this was happening too fast for me to process.

"I'm sure he talked to Jane, and she probably told him. I don't know. But, at any rate, it gives you an excuse to get rid of him to search for her. Hold on to Dash, and keep him here with you." Then he shoved off from the tree and sprinted into the thick woods.

Fortunately, I'd grabbed onto Dash's collar. He rewarded me with a howl of protest.

"I want to help Nice Guy," Dash pleaded.

"How? He has a plan, and you aren't part of it," I said, although Will's plan made no sense to me.

Dash strained against my hold, but his twenty-pound effort gained him nothing. "He's in trouble!" he protested like he, Prince Dasher Dangerdog Bean, was the only creature that could help. I had to admit, he had an overabundance of confidence.

"Possibly, but the best way to help Will right now is to do what he asked. So, in case you were too distracted by his pocketful of treats, he was very clear. You need to stay here with me," I stressed clearly and forcefully. Besides, even though Will could be charming, I didn't trust him, and I wasn't letting him near Dash. As it was, I suspected that Dash's whole motivation was to stay with Honey. I had to get her back.

Dash sat down with what sounded like a huff. Can dogs huff? I suppose if a dog can talk, he can also huff. Anyway,

Dash gave up his struggle, but I didn't let him go in case he was trying to trick me. I wouldn't put anything past this clever dachshund.

I felt a cool breeze whisk by.

"Heads up," Audrey said. "Brooksby is headed your way with his I-mean-business expression."

Thankful for the warning, I made a plan and decided to throw him off by killing him with kindness. If *that* was even a remote possibility.

With Dash nestled in my arms, I pasted a broad smile on my face and turned around. "Hello, Officer Brooksby. We meet again."

## 18

Dash snarled and struggled to leap out of my arms. Not helpful.

"Put me down, Nikki. He smells evil. I don't like his type."

"It's okay, Dash," I said. "Settle down. I've got this."

Birdie, scurrying close behind Brooksby, soon caught up, her flaming red hair glowing like a crown of fire. She said in a high-pitched sing-song voice, "Officer Brooksby." She was up to something. "I have chocolate chip pecan cookies fresh from the oven. Right now, they're melt in your mouth perfection, sooo," she dragged it out. "How about we go inside before they get cold."

I almost laughed out loud at Birdie's blatant bribe. From his oversized belly, I suspected her offer hit him in his vulnerable spot.

In fact, his expression did soften. He licked his lips and patted his protruding gut. I half expected to see drool drip from his mouth. If I had to guess, I'd say Birdie had experience using her delicious baking to get his attention.

"How about," Brooksby said as if he was struggling to

spit out his thought, "you bring a plate of those cookies out here, Birdie. That way, it won't look like I went inside where someone could accuse me of taking a bribe. Nothing wrong with sitting right out here by the fish pond while we talk. And if a warm, delicious cookie lands right next to me, well, no one would think it odd if I had one. Or two. You know, to be polite."

"It's not a bribe if we're outside? That doesn't make a lick of sense," Dash said. "Quick! Birdie's leaving! Remind her to bring me a treat, too. I'm sure that mangy swamp monster of a detective won't share a chocolate chip pecan cookie with me."

"Never mind that dogs can't have chocolate, Dash."

"Tell Birdie. Tell her! She's almost in the house!" Dash frantically yelled at me.

Poor Dash. "Only if you promise to behave," I whispered to my wiggling companion.

Immediately, he settled like a limp bag of laundry and licked my chin. "I promise," he said, turning into a docile well-trained dog. Interesting. He could behave when he wanted something.

"Birdie!" I yelled. "Don't forget something for Dash."

She gave a thumbs up and disappeared inside.

"Happy now?" I said, out of Brooksby's earshot.

"Thank you, Nikki. You're the best. Now, sit down and find out what that mangy swamp monster wants."

I walked toward the pansy-shaped chairs around the koi pond. "Be careful," Audrey whispered. "Brooksby is up to something."

No kidding. He certainly hadn't stopped by for a friendly chat over cookies and milk. Even if he couldn't resist Birdie's cookies, I was positive he didn't have a friendly chat on his agenda.

When I reached the pond, I said in my friendliest voice, "Officer Brooksby, please have a seat; make yourself comfortable." I almost gagged at my syrupy sweet voice. But, if I had to play the welcome-to-my-home hostess to get what I wanted, I'd pull it off like a champ.

He warily looked at Dash and took a step back. I suppose I couldn't blame him, based on Dash's earlier attempt to snack on his finger.

I laughed like it was nothing. "Don't worry about this little guy. He settled in here like it's been his home forever. To be honest, I'm surprised at how quickly Dash made himself comfortable, but maybe he was just confused this morning when we saw you. Put yourself in his paws—abandoned, rescued, new people. It's a lot for any pooch."

Brooksby didn't look convinced. He backed away a few inches more, causing him to bump up against one of the chairs. The seat caught him in the back of his knees, and down he went with a thud. At least he landed in the pansy chair and not on the grass. I sat down before he decided he'd had enough of this nonsense.

Audrey's laugh sounded like a whisper through dry leaves, but Brooksby was too distracted to notice anything out of the ordinary. On the other hand, Dash jumped off my lap and went straight for Brooksby's shoes. From the look on his face, I thought the poor man might faint away. Or, pull out his gun and threaten Dash. Or me to get control of him. Thankfully, he did neither, or we would have had a war on our hands.

Dash, oblivious to the scene he'd caused, thoroughly sniffed the soles of Brooksby's shoes. When he finished, he said, "He smells like Honey's cage at the shelter, Nikki. What was he doing there?" He sniffed some more. "And something else... sticky cinnamon stuff stuck on his shoe."

Uh-oh. Honey's kennel where Clive had been assaulted, and now he was here? This couldn't be good. But it did make sense since Jane called the police. The cinnamon stuff? Probably from a daily donut addiction.

Birdie arrived carrying Audrey's antique silver tray. She'd once told me the rose-patterned tray was a wedding present from some elderly aunt. I knew she loved it dearly from all the times she'd polished it for special occasions. I wasn't sure this was that kind of special occasion, but apparently, Birdie was out to impress. Or distract with whatever tools she had on hand.

She set it on the wrought iron table next to Brooksby, cleverly angled, so the deep moonlight blue plate—another prized procession—with the biggest, most chocolate chip-filled cookie was oh, so close to his pudgy fingers. An irresistible morsel to be sure.

Without a moment's hesitation, Brooksby snatched that cookie like he was afraid someone else might beat him to it.

I cleared my throat to cover a laugh.

Dash, however, showed his complete lack of self-control when he shouted, "Where's *my* cookie? Don't let him eat mine, too! He looks like he has a bottomless pit for a stomach."

He pawed at Brooksby's leg. He lifted them out of Dash's reach, bumping the table in the process. The tray slid dangerously close to tipping over the edge, but I lunged just in time, catching the tray and corralling Dash back in my lap. It was quite the feat if I didn't say so myself.

"What's with that dog?"

"He has a big personality," I said and reached for the dog treat before Dash wiggled free and landed smack in the middle of the tray.

"Here you go, Dash."

I put him down and tossed the dog bone on the ground, well away from Brooksby, hoping Dash would behave as he'd promised. Brooksby grabbed another cookie, the first long gone.

"Iced tea?" Birdie asked. "It's Audrey's special blend of peach with a hint of honey." She handed him a tall glass. He shoved the cookie in his mouth, crumbs spewing out as he accepted the tea. Condensation dripped off the glass onto his pants on top of the crumbs. His attempt to sweep the mess off his lap resulted in a mash of crumbs, partly melted chocolate chips, and water smearing into a big dark stain. I almost felt sorry for him.

Instead of pity, though, I took advantage of his full mouth and decided this was a good time for me to take charge of the situation before it went completely off the rails.

"I met your grandson at the Underdog Animal Shelter today," I said. "He..."

And just like that, Brooksby's eyes narrowed into slits, effectively stopping my thoughts dead in their tracks. He put his glass on the tray with a loud clatter. Gone was the bumbling, clumsy man with an appetite like a hippo. Somehow, he'd transformed into a shrewd officer of the law.

"So, Ms. Knight, you were at the shelter." His icy glare held me paralyzed as I realized I'd walked right into a dangerous trap.

Without the help of any notes and with his eyes boring into me he said, "Ms. Knight, supposedly you arrived here in Frog Hollow this morning. You found a dog who just happened to belong to a murder victim. You and your..."

He paused for a breath and glanced at Birdie before his next barrage. "Er...friend spontaneously drove by the scene of that murder. Your car is covered with scratches. And now you admit you were at the Underdog Animal Shelter, scene of another murder attempt. In my lengthy career, that adds up to more coincidences than are remotely possible. Now, I have one question, and I suggest you answer truthfully."

My hands dripped with sweat. My heart pounded. I took a deep breath in and slowly exhaled to calm my nerves and keep my thoughts hidden from this shrewd man.

"Of course, Officer Brooksby," I said.

I'd be as truthful as possible under the circumstances.

## 19

Officer Brooksby crossed one ankle onto his knee and leaned back against the back of the chair like he was settling in for a long visit. He drummed his fingers on the top of the table, then picked up his iced tea and took a long drink.

This strategy was designed, I assumed, to make me sweat with worry. I was sweating for sure because it was hot and humid, but it actually gave me time to plan how to throw him off his game. I'd already hit him with kindness, now, I'd blindside him with the unexpected.

Audrey swirled behind Brooksby, back and forth, like a frustrated mom impatiently waiting on the sideline of a life or death final contest.

I leaned forward wearing my in-charge persona—direct eye contact, even breath. With a strong voice, I said, "Your grandson is a very committed person. When I talked to him he made it clear he's extremely devoted to the shelter animals. Probably all animals. Officer Brooksby, can I ask you a question?"

Brooksby clenched his jaw. He studied my face with all

the intent of someone weighing his options. Neutralizing my expression—a steady but not aggressive gaze and minimal blinking—I masked my internal turmoil.

Finally, he said, "Okay, Ms. Knight. One question."

His response sounded like an indulgent parent who already knew the question, answer, and follow-up.

"Where is your grandson now?"

He looked startled. A slight jerk of his shoulders, but he recovered quickly. Yet I knew I'd just hit him with the last question he expected from me. I helped myself to a cookie, then fake swooned and licked my lips to show Brooksby I didn't have a care in the world except enjoying Birdie's baking delights.

"Why do you care?' he sputtered.

Yes! Welcome to my trap, said the spider. Brooksby had walked into my opening.

"Well," I said. "When I went to the shelter, Will was more than helpful, but based on the multiple times the front bell rang, a busy stretch of people kept coming and going. Will left me with one of the dogs in the exercise yard when he had to leave to take care of any potential adopters. The next thing I knew, Jane joined me there. She said she'd been talking to you and learned that I'd rescued Prince Dasher Dangerdog Bean when he'd been left at the gas station."

That may have been more information than they'd discussed, but it was all accurate.

Brooksby nodded, but it was a slow nod indicating he had no idea where all my rambling was headed.

"Well, I told Jane I wanted to adopt Honey. She's one of the shelter dogs. When we walked inside, we discovered her employee slumped in one of the kennels." I batted my eyelashes in a show of innocence before my next question. "What can you tell me about Clive Martin?"

I was on a roll and wondered how far I'd get before Brooksby pushed back.

His chin went up, and his scowl deepened.

"Listen here, Ms. Knight. That's about all the patience I have for your shenanigans." I got my answer with a burst of anger added. "You asked where my grandson is now. That's exactly what I came here to find out. According to Jane Cross, you left the scene of a crime with one of the shelter dogs. A dog that I know my grandson was very attached to. A dog that I've been informed you have no adoption papers for. How do you explain that?" He looked around. "Where is Honey? What are you and my grandson up to?"

That was way more than the one question he'd said he had for me, but I took the high road and didn't point out the discrepancy.

"Nothing at all, Officer Brooksby. I have no idea what you're talking about," I said. "Jane Cross asked me to take Honey because she couldn't very well put the poor dog back in her kennel with all the blood and an injured man inside." I stood up, enjoying this height advantage. "As a matter of fact, Honey ran off just before you arrived, and I was about to search for her. So, if you don't have any more questions, I think finding a lost dog takes precedence over anything else right now."

I glanced at Birdie, nodding enthusiastically. Dash paced back and forth in front of me.

"Find Honey. Yes!" he said, heading toward the stone wall.

"A lost dog does *not* take precedence over murder and attempted murder, Ms. Knight. Let me ask you one more time. Do you know where Will is?"

"I do not," I answered and stared right back at him

without any guilty conscience because it was the truth. "Are you suggesting that he's a suspect?"

"I'm suggesting that you'd better not be hiding anything connected to these crimes, Ms. Knight. I'm suggesting that the only people that we know were at the shelter were you, my grandson, and the victim. Ever since you arrived back in town, everything has been turned upside down. Something fishy is going on, and you better believe I'll get to the bottom of it." He grabbed another cookie, stood up, and stomped across the lawn without a proper thank you or goodbye.

"Brooksby's mamma would be very disappointed with his lack of manners," I said quietly enough so only Birdie and Audrey would possibly hear.

They both snorted, then a whoosh next to the koi pond announced Audrey's arrival near me even before she made herself visible.

As if I had absolutely zilch to worry about, she gave a wave of her luminous arm and said, "He's got nothing, or he would have brought you in for questioning."

Maybe he had nothing right now, but he was looking for something, which didn't bode well for me. Not that I'd committed any crime except for removing—I hated to say stealing—items from a murder victim's car. That in itself gave me no choice but to stay ahead of this mess before I got tied to these victims and went down like a sinking ship.

"Nikki," Birdie said and walked over, wrapping me in one of her big tight don't-worry-about-anything hugs. "You were absolutely amazing. Brooksby had no idea what hit him once you got rolling." She shook her head, chuckling as if it was the best show ever.

I loved the compliments, but I still had a lot of work to do. "You softened him up for me, Birdie. Those cookies," I rolled my eyes toward heaven, "and the iced tea… a brilliant diversion!"

"I knew you'd get the hang of this investigation stuff, Niks," Audrey added. "Now," she clapped her hands, silent as always, "we need to search Clive's house for clues."

"What?" I said, incredulous at her lack of concern for me breaking the law.

"What's *your* next step then?" she asked.

I had to think about that. "I have to find Honey before I do anything else." Was I just putting off the inevitable? Hopefully, Honey had found a safe haven with Will. And if I found him? Then what? Adding more people to our investigation party only increased the chances of someone uncovering the truth about Audrey and Dash.

While I hemmed and hawed, Will stepped over the stone wall onto the grass; Honey bolted past him and charged toward me. Her enthusiastic jump caught me by surprise and practically knocked me over. Dash joined in the melee, which was the tipping point to knock me onto my butt. Both dogs licked and squirmed until I rolled out from under them and managed to stand up, laughing at their antics.

After all that, I glanced at Will again. He stood frozen in place, staring at the spot where Audrey had been before he stepped onto the lawn. Had he seen her?

"Will Brooksby," Birdie said, breaking him out of his self-induced spell. "You look hot and sweaty. Come over here and help yourself to my special pecan chocolate chip cookies and a big glass of iced tea."

She nudged the tray, which caught Will's attention, just as Birdie must have planned. "Then sit yourself down," she added.

"Yeah," Will said. "It is hot. I must be a little dehydrated because I thought I saw," he paused and shook his head like he was trying to dislodge something, "a ghost by the pond."

Birdie laughed. "No worries, Will. I think that almost every day, at least since Audrey died," she said with a voice that cracked with emotion. Even though Audrey was still around in her ghostly form, it wasn't the same. Birdie obviously missed her dearly. As did I.

"I chalk it up to wishful thinking," Birdie said softly. She patted the chair where Will's granddad had been sitting. "Now, sit down and tell us everything you know about Clive Martin."

I couldn't wait to hear this.

## 20

Will slumped down onto one of the pansy chairs, just as Birdie had suggested. The metal flower petals making up the back of the chair hugged his body like it was designed just for him. The chairs had a way of doing that, I'd noticed.

He glanced around, still checking for ghosts I suspected, but he must have decided either they were gone or his mind had played a trick on him. He let out a deep sigh and his body slowly relaxed into the comfortable spot.

Audrey, as she did in situations like this, had disappeared from view, though I was sure she had picked a spot nearby to keep an eye on everything. The problem with her new ghost gig, I realized, was that she couldn't truly be with us when we had company.

Oh, sure, she hovered in the background and sometimes made objects fall over or created an unexpected breeze now and then, but basically, she had to stay out of sight. She couldn't add her wise wisdom or snarky sayings to the conversation whenever she felt like it. I missed that.

But on the plus side, I had a new-found freedom to take

charge. That being said, this new order created pressures and responsibilities surrounding my decisions.

While sitting here by the koi pond with Will and Birdie and pondering this new revelation, I realized that I rather enjoyed this new role. Listening, learning, and discovering clues was an adventure I hadn't planned on, but with my normal nosiness and suspicious nature, it suited me well.

"Nikki!" Birdie's stern voice brought me back to the conversation. "Did you hear what Will just said?"

Oops! Apparently, I had to hone my listening skills, or the learning and discovering parts would suffer.

"Sorry," I mumbled. "You were telling us about Clive Martin."

Will rolled his eyes like I was a ditzy female and helped himself to a cookie. He'd replaced his shocked expression with a cocky grin, which made him look like he thought *he* was in charge. We'd see about that.

His attitude annoyed me. But I heard Audrey's voice in my head reminding me to keep my feelings to myself. For the sake of educating myself, I did just that.

"Clive Martin is involved with some shady characters," Will said. "I didn't tell you before at the shelter because I was afraid someone might hear me. I had to keep up a front. I was there to take care of the animals and stay out of everyone's business."

My take on that? Will Brooksby was a scheming, egotistical, untrustworthy…

"Nikki! Pay attention. What is it with you?" Birdie asked. She poured a glass of iced tea. "Here," she said, pressing it into my hand. "I think the heat is getting to you."

It wasn't the heat, it was Will's sneaky behavior, but I wasn't about to say that out loud. Instead, I smiled. "You were saying?" I said and sipped the tea.

"Right." Will continued with much less enthusiasm than when he'd started. "You have Dash now, and I think somehow he's connected to all this. The shelter, Vernon, Clive." He swept his hand in a wide gesture to include all of them. "I don't know how, but that's why I came here. Since you're connected, I hope you'll help me figure out what's going on."

He put his glass down and leaned forward with both elbows on his knees. "From what I overheard, I think Vernon and Clive were working together on something. I saw Vernon hand Clive a bag. Clive grinned and slapped him on the shoulder and said, 'Jane's happy, I'm happy. All's good.' After that, Vernon left with Dash."

"Okay," I said. No surprise there. It matched Audrey's account of eavesdropping on them in town before I'd arrived. But what was Jane happy about? If Will's information was even true.

"You aren't shocked?" he asked and abruptly stood up. "I think I've made a terrible mistake."

"Don't let him leave, Nikki! He'll take Honey," Dash shouted.

"I'm sure Jane would be more comfortable with me in charge of these two dogs. Come on, Prince Dasher, Honey," Will said. "We have work to do."

"Stop!" I said after Dash gave my calf a nip. I meant the command for Dash, but Will stopped in his tracks. I couldn't explain my outburst except to say, "Don't get all huffy, Will. Sit down and tell us more."

Of course, Dash thought I'd taken his advice, this dachshund who spent more time yelling at me than behaving like a calm companion. He acted like I was his servant. Great. The two of us had a few things to straighten out. Later, though.

Will looked at me with his steady German shepherd-type assessment. This time, shrewd and calculating. I half-expected him to add a growl. He didn't.

"You're acting weird. Are you working with Clive?" he asked.

"Of course not!" I ran my fingers through my hair in frustration. "It's been a strange day, but I think we might have common goals." Did we?

Though Birdie covered her mouth with her hand, an unmistakable chuckle escaped. She was enjoying this conflict way too much. I could only imagine the thoughts roiling through Audrey's imaginative mind. She probably wished she could give me a good shove and tell me to get going with the investigation.

"Such as?" Will asked. His raised brows indicated a strong skepticism. Of course, he knew nothing about the root of my odd behavior–my ghost and talking dog. I wouldn't share those details under any circumstance.

I arched one brow. "Such as finding out who killed Vernon and attacked Clive before your grandfather links one of us to this whole messy situation," I said.

Will abruptly sat down. Honey lay her head in his lap, and he lost his long fingers in her fur.

"Now I'm intrigued. I know my grandfather has been looking for me, but you think he has his eyes on *you*? Interesting."

"Because of Dash. I mean, I found Dash abandoned at the gas station before I ever heard of Vernon or knew he'd been murdered. But..."

"Tell him, Nikki. Tell him we found the body. And tell him about the cats."

"What's wrong with Prince Dasher?" Will asked. "He's acting very upset."

"Yeah, he does that whenever he hears Vernon's name." I gave Dash a remember-our-agreement-to-behave-yourself look and shushed him. "Do you think Dash could be a target?"

"I don't know."

"The cats, Nikki. Tell him about the cats."

I cast a quick side-eye at Birdie, but she gave me a barely noticeable shake of her head. I wasn't sure what she was thinking, but I hadn't planned to confide any details with Will anyway.

"Here's what I propose," I said. "This day feels like it has lasted longer than a year. The police will be everywhere now, so how about we regroup tomorrow?" Was that general enough?

Birdie clapped her hands together. "Come for breakfast, Will. The more company, the better. In case you didn't know, that's my favorite meal. Will, you know Lacey Dawson, don't you? She owns the Shear Magic hair salon in town, and she'll be here for breakfast, too. She's such a hard-working young woman. Nikki and Lacey go way back."

As Birdie babbled away, I noticed Will's eyes widen and his nose flare when she mentioned Lacey's name.

"Okay," he said and stood up. I wasn't sure if he'd agreed to come or just needed an excuse for ending the conversation. I was fine with him *not* coming. "Now I have to talk to my grandfather before he sends the whole department out to find me."

Dash nudged Honey. She followed him to the far side of the koi pond, where they both got lost in some interesting smell. I recognized the little dashie's tactics. This time his distraction helped me big time. Jane told me to take care of Honey, and that's exactly what I planned to do. Will took her before, and thankfully, he returned with her, but now I'd keep her right here with us at Moonlight Mansion. No ifs, ands, or buts about it.

Will looked at Honey, opened his mouth, and then changed his mind. Without another word, he stepped over the stone wall and disappeared into the woods.

"Good," Dash said. "He's gone. I used to like him, but today he smelled like something out of the dumpster."

All I cared about at the moment was eating Birdie's fried chicken, flopping onto my soft bed, and slipping into a deep dreamless night's sleep.

Was that too much to ask for after the day I'd had?

I held no delusions that tomorrow wouldn't bring new surprises.

## 21

I opened my eyes to bright sunshine streaming through the bedroom window. Crystals hanging from the sash threw rainbows that moved across the floor and around the walls. Glorious!

I stretched. First, one arm, then the other in a slow, lazy wake-up for my muscles.

"I'm hungry. Get up!" Dash yelled in a whiny desperate, I'm-starving voice.

Right. Everything flooded back from the day before.

"Dash?" I said in a gentle tone. "Is that how you spoke to your family before they sent you to the shelter?"

"I guess so."

"That explains everything," I mumbled, realizing I had a monumental task ahead. Time to teach him to mend his ways.

"What do you mean? Are you sending me back? You can't do that. I chose you, Nikki. We can talk to each other." He babbled and paced next to my bed like I'd really rattled him.

I sat up and dangled my feet over the edge of the bed.

Dash sat on the floor staring at me with the saddest puppy dog eyes I'd ever seen. The kind of look that tears at your heart and squeezes until you have no choice but to sigh and let go of your annoyance.

I reached down with both hands and gently lifted him up next to Honey, still fast asleep on the bed.

"I'm not sending you back, Dash. Ever. I promise." He licked my hand, and his tail thumped on the blankets. "But, tone it down a little. Stop with all the demands. If we're going to be a team, you have to respect me instead of acting like I'm your servant."

"But, I've always had someone who jumped whenever I needed something." He sounded genuinely puzzled.

"Let me put it another way. You love Honey. That's obvious because you treat her like she's special. And she is. But, the rest of us in this house are special, too. Does that make sense?"

He sat as still as a statue. "You want me to treat you like a piece of yummy sausage?" He sniffed the air. "I smell sausage."

I burst out laughing. Dash was his own brand of special, but he was still a dog with a short attention span, which was usually centered on food.

"Not exactly what I meant, but we'll work on this," I said. If I was sure of anything, I'd be working on Dash's behavior for as long as we were together. And, I hoped that was a very long time. Besides, this wasn't necessarily a bad thing since we could both learn from each other. My expectation, though, was that more of me rubbed off on Dash than vice versa.

"Come on, Honey. I'll race you to the sausage," Dash said, impatient now for me to open the door.

I did, and Dash raced off. Honey leaped off the bed right

behind him. They clattered down the stairs from my third-floor apartment, leaving me with a few minutes of peace and quiet. Maybe.

"Nice speech, Niks," Audrey said, floating into my room. So much for peace and quiet. "Dash certainly likes to push your buttons."

She laughed, and I joined in.

Audrey was right. It was a good reminder that his comments could only bother me if I let them. Note to self: *ignore the dachshund; he doesn't know any better.*

In her effortless way, Audrey moved to the window to look out at the gorgeous view of her garden and koi pond below. This, after all, had been her space until the fateful fall off the balcony.

"I'm glad you're here now, Niks. You're the only one who will love this place as I did; who will care for the roses and peonies and lilacs properly."

She twirled around, her gauzy dress flying behind her like a cloud until she faced me. "But you must solve this murder, so Brooksby doesn't have a chance to tarnish your reputation. He'd love that, you know. For him, it would be like getting even with me."

"Even?"

She turned back to the view. "You probably didn't know this, but Moonlight Mansion used to belong to his parents. Way back when Brooksby and I were sixteen, his parents had money problems. Huge problems. About to lose everything kind of problems."

This memory sounded like it came from a distant place.

"What's that got to do with you?" I didn't know where this was going, but I suspected I was about to hear a bad ending for someone.

"Brooksby's parents saw me as an easy target—a just-turned-sixteen girl flush with money from a trust fund. So, they made a proposal. One they thought was a guaranteed win and a way out of their money troubles."

She paused, maybe unsure if she wanted to share this difficult bit of her history. I held my breath and waited.

"In exchange for clearing up all their debts, they made a bet. And lost. They lost Moonlight Mansion to *me*, Niks. They gambled that I couldn't beat Brooksby in a race from here to the center of town and back, about five miles. If I lost, I agreed to pay off their debts from the trust fund. If I *won*," she threw up her hands in a wild gesture, "the mansion became mine."

"Why on earth did you do it?" I was completely dumbfounded at the risk she took.

"The trust fund was huge. It's not like I was going to the poorhouse if I lost and," she stared out the window for what felt like an hour but was only a minute or so, "I'd always loved this mansion. Plus," she turned to face me, "I had all the confidence in the world that I could win. I wasn't a hundred percent sure, but close to it."

"So, you and Bud Brooksby ran against each other." This thought boggled my mind. After all, I knew Brooksby now as an overweight slug but Audrey had always been slim, trim, and super athletic.

"I know what you're thinking, Niks, but Brooksby was a top athlete as a teen. The star runner on the track team at the time, as a matter of fact. But that's only because girls weren't allowed to compete back then," she said, tooting her own horn.

"Anyhow, I guess you could say his parents were a tad overconfident. Some said cocky. Seemed they were one hundred percent positive their grandson couldn't lose, especially to a girl. They joked that they'd pulled something over the naïve, wealthy, spoiled, and over-confident Audrey Knight. Well, Niks, that was all I needed to hear. I got so riled up, no way I planned to lose. I'd show them what *this* girl was made of." She shrugged as if, after all these years, it was no longer a big deal.

"And, as is so often the case, Brooksby's parents were wrong. And the message from my story is that Brooksby is wrong about you too, Niks. You have to show him that. We have to find clues that will keep your good name free and clear from his monkey business. You're back here in Frog Hollow, and you have to be the..."

"Baddest girl around," we said in unison and laughed.

"Right. But in the best most honest way, Niks. You have to be tough but smart. Bull-headed sometimes but trustworthy always. Clever without showing your hand. And I know that's you through and through."

Thankful for the confidence and brimming with a cool conviction that I *would* live up to the whole kit and caboodle, a warm glow settled over me. But before I got too sidetracked, I needed to clear up one detail. "I have one question. How did you beat Brooksby?"

Audrey smiled. "I was faster," she said like it was her greatest life achievement.

"But no one thought you had a ghost of a chance to win."

A tremor went through Audrey's body as if she'd just been shocked. "People accused me of cheating, Niks. Brooksby spread rumors about me, which is why he and I have never gotten along. But that has nothing to do with you, and it needs to stop. Now. That happened more than fifty years ago."

She paused as the sun streamed through and around her, turning her into a sort of glowing vision. Then, she continued, "My fear, Niks, is that Will still carries this feud and wants revenge for his grandfather. I hope I'm wrong, but I just don't know."

Audrey sounded devastated about leaving this legacy on my doorstep. Rather than on the doorstep of Moonlight Mansion. But as far as I was concerned, Will had nothing over me, and I'd watch him like a retriever with both eyes on a pheasant in a bush. If he thought he could ruin me, I'd beat him to the finish line and prove him wrong just like Audrey beat Bud.

Audrey spun around and signaled an end to this topic. "So, Niks, what's your plan for today?"

"I'm not sure yet." I pulled a clean t-shirt on and found my favorite black shorts. "I am curious to know why Birdie invited both Will and Lacey for breakfast. What's she up to?" I wiggled into my shorts and snapped them closed, then looked under my bed for my sandals.

"You didn't get to see how they usually act when they're together, but when Lacey comes over to do Birdie's hair, those two women gossip about everything from recipes to dating. Birdie knows that Lacey is infatuated with Will."

I looked at Audrey, somewhat surprised to hear this. "She's playing matchmaker?"

"Ha! Far from that, Niks. Birdie wants to protect Lacey."

I snagged my sandals and dragged them out from under the bed. "Funny way to do that," I mumbled. There was so much I didn't understand, and I added Birdie's protective attitude to that list.

"She wants to keep him close, make him comfortable, let him reveal his hand. Or, that's the plan, at least. The thing is, Brooksby and Will could be working together."

I plopped onto my bed and let that sink it. It didn't take much pondering. "Like good cop/bad cop? Except in this case, it's more like good grandson/bad grandfather." Maybe my gut feeling about Will was right all along. Under that handsome veneer, he had an agenda that included me in a bad way.

Audrey smiled with satisfaction. "Exactly. You learn quickly. There's one more complication to this theory."

"What? Will is really a vampire and needs my blood to survive because I'm descended from a ghost?" If that ended up being the case, I might just leave Frog Hollow forever.

"Worse than that, Niks."

"Worse? I'm not sure that's possible." I slipped my feet into my sandals and sat up straight, worried about where this was going.

"According to the terms of the deed when I took over Moonlight Mansion, I had to live here until I died."

Okay, I thought. Done and dusted. Then Audrey added the kicker.

"And upon my death," she added with a cautious pause, "the heir of my choosing had to move in within six months and live here forever."

I blinked my shock.

"You are my heir of choice, and you've moved in well within that timeframe. But, here's the catch. If for any reason, you stop living here, the deed reverts to Brooksby or his heir of choice. That person is Will."

That hit me like a bomb exploding in my head. "Like if I'm in jail?"

"Yes, Niks. Anything."

"Over my dead body!" Determination mixed with fury led to a level of resolve I'd never felt before. I'd do absolutely everything possible to get to the bottom of this before anyone took Moonlight Mansion away from me.

"That's what I'm so worried about, Niks."

## 22

Birdie's kitchen smelled wonderful. Like always.

Mornings had always been my favorite time to venture into her kitchen because it always got the day started with a smile. Freshly ground coffee, bacon, sausage, pecan muffins, and whatever main course she'd planned filled the mansion and my nose with drooling delicious anticipation.

"What took you so long, Nikki?" Dash asked when I entered. "I tried to save you a sausage. I really did, but somehow they're all gone." He licked his chops.

Interestingly, Dash didn't look the least bit upset about the empty sausage platter on the counter or the bulge in his stomach.

Birdie snorted as she balanced muffins on one arm and a plate of bacon on the other and successfully navigated between Dash and Honey shamelessly begging for more. Fortunately, this batch of goodies arrived safely at the table.

"What did that bottomless piggy just tell you?" Birdie asked after she'd unloaded her offerings.

"Piggy? Did Birdie just call me a piggy? Those sausages

were fair game, Nikki. They slid off the plate and fell on the floor. I cleaned up her mess. Birdie should thank *me*!" He waddled to the water bowl, drank most of it, then proceeded to the door. "I need to go out."

"Please?" I said. This was as good a time as any to work on his manners.

"Please." He scratched at the door. "Hurry. Please."

I opened the door, and both dogs darted past me, Honey jumping over Dash and taking the lead.

"Stay in the yard!" I yelled. There was enough on my agenda today without worrying about lost dogs.

"I'll keep an eye on them. Smelling all this food is kind of painful," Audrey said sadly as she floated outside.

"Good morning!" Lacey sang out in her high, super friendly voice. "I let myself in; hope you don't mind." She dropped a big canvas bag on the floor, walked to the table, and helped herself to a piece of bacon. It disappeared in three crunchy bites. "I'm afraid I'll have to eat and run. One of my best customers called with an emergency hair situation. You don't know her, Nikki, but she has," Lacey held up her fingers in quotation marks, "an emergency at least once a week. But, a customer is a customer." She settled onto a chair at the table and reached for a muffin. "Where are the dogs? I brought treats."

"Perfect," I said. "That will get them back in the house before they follow something into the woods." I walked to the door and hollered, "Lacey brought treats!"

Honey arrived like an eagle swooping in to catch a salmon, but Dash had disappeared. I ran outside, positive he'd taken off, and scanned the yard everywhere for him. Audrey whispered, "He's fine, just a little slow with that full belly dragging on the ground. And, thanks for giving me a head's up that Lacey arrived. Is Will here, too?"

"Haven't seen him yet." Then, I spotted Dash practically dragging himself to the house with a few grunts added in for sympathy, judging from the sad look in his eyes.

"A little help, please. I hurt my foot, Nikki."

"Your foot, huh?" I doubted that excuse but picked him up and carried him inside anyway because I did feel sorry for the entitled dachshund. I couldn't expect to fix all of his bad habits in a day. The please didn't hurt, either.

"On my blanket, please, Nikki, "he whimpered. "I need to rest my foot."

I obliged and checked his feet, just in case. As I suspected, each paw looked perfectly fine, but if he needed an excuse to hide his eating problem, so be it. I'd work on that another day. Unless he'd learned to monitor his portions on his own—the hard way.

"So," I heard Lacey say after I made Dash comfortable. "I passed Will on my way over here. He was pulled off on the side of the road. On his phone," she said in between bites of a luscious veggie cheese omelet and crunches of toast.

"Car trouble?" I asked. That might explain why he hadn't arrived yet. I poured a mug of coffee and slipped onto a chair across from Lacey.

"No. He was on his motorcycle, but that wasn't the problem. When I slowed down to see if he needed help, he waved me on like I was an annoying gnat. Didn't even bother to say hello."

Lacey sounded aggravated. "But I did hear him say to whoever was on the other end of the phone call, 'Sure, I'll visit Clive right now.' I wonder what that's about?"

I helped myself to one of Birdie's pecan muffins and mulled over that bit of information. "That tells us a couple of things," I said, then bit into the moist, sweet, crunchy pastry.

"Yeah, that he's rude and thinks he's a hotshot," Lacey said.

"Okay, I'll agree with you there, but he isn't hiding out from the law, so maybe he's not a suspect for attacking Clive. And, he's planning to go to the hospital. Why visit someone he doesn't like? What's the motivation for that?"

"And," Birdie raised her finger, "he's blowing off breakfast here. Who in their right mind would ever miss out on one of my famous breakfast spreads?"

Lacey choked on her last bite of toast. I rushed around the table to pat her back until she held up her hands and muttered, "Stop. I'm fine. Why'd you invite Will here for breakfast, Birdie? You aren't trying to play matchmaker, are you? Because I told you I don't need any help. I manage to muck up every relationship all on my own. Not that there's any," the air quotes popped up again, "relationship with Will Brooksby."

Birdie's face actually turned the same red as her new hair color. "Hardly. I'm trying to protect you from jumping into... all I'll say is you know how I feel about Will. I'd hoped," she seemed to be choosing her words carefully, "that having him sit here outnumbered by Nikki, you, and me might bring out his true colors—good or bad. I guess you got a glimpse of his real personality when he waved you on."

"Yeah, well, a girl can dream even if Will is way out of my league." Lacey carried her empty plate and coffee mug to the sink, turned around, and faced me. "You're more his type, Nikki."

My jaw dropped. She'd obviously gotten the wrong message from Birdie, or she preferred to stick her head in the sand when it came to her attraction for the handsome Will Brooksby.

A quick swish of Audrey's shimmering gown caught my attention at the corner of my eye. It reminded me of our earlier conversation about the Brooksby feud and how Will might be out for revenge.

"Will is definitely not my type, Lacey. Besides, if he's such a decent guy, why did he blow off breakfast here this morning? If he couldn't make it, the least he could have done was let Birdie know. I, for one, am not losing a lick of sleep over a no-show. And as far as Will's behavior is concerned," I said, hoping I wasn't about to step over some invisible line with my next comment, but I had to wake her up. "You should be careful around someone who seems to focus on himself."

Would Lacey finally hear that we were trying to warn her to be careful?

"We'll see," Lacey said. "Will is complicated. But deep down, I think he's decent and just needs the right woman to fix his flaws. Thanks for being honest, Nikki. I'm thrilled that you aren't interested in grabbing him for yourself."

I wanted to bury my head in my hands or shake some sense into her, but it was obvious I couldn't change Lacey's mind. And, if she thought she could fix his flaws, she had a lot more to learn about the opposite sex than I could teach her.

She grabbed a muffin. "For the road," she said, flourishing the muffin in the air. "I've gotta step on it and get to my salon. Poor Mrs. Sweeney will keel over right on my doorstep if she has to wait for one second. Listen, Nikki, stop in later, and I'll give you that trim, and we can chat about, you know," she lowered her voice to a conspiratorial whisper, "working together on this case." She hefted her canvas bag off the floor and left the way she'd come.

"It's hopeless." Birdie sighed. "I've been trying to tell

Lacey that Will won't make her happy in the long run. Based on the track record of the men in his background, he just isn't the type. Lacey is convinced that she's the perfect woman to change him."

I knew she had a futile plan, but this wasn't the time to let my mind wander to the what ifs of my past love life.

Audrey moved around the table in her shimmering way. "No loss. It's best Will didn't show up this morning. Now Niks can get down to the business of finding out who killed Vernon."

I swiped the last of the egg off my plate with my toast and savored the peppery, crunchy bite.

"I'm going to the hospital," I announced with confidence.

"Interesting first stop," Birdie said. "Who exactly are you hoping to bump into?"

I stood up and carried my plate to the sink. Then, before I answered, I packed up a half dozen of Birdie's delicious muffins in a paper bag. "I'm keeping an open mind about that."

I looked at her with a confident grin on my face and tucked the bag under my arm. "One thing I can count on, though, it'll be a worthwhile visit."

## 23

Of course, Audrey insisted on coming with me to the hospital. Truth be told, I didn't mind. I liked the advantage of having another set of eyes and ears privy to places I couldn't see and conversations I couldn't hear. If one had to be a ghost, invisibility was a big plus. I didn't let myself dwell on the fact that first, you had to die in order to gain this particular talent, though.

Dash? He jumped in the car before I could stop him. He let me know that under no uncertain terms, would he let me leave him behind this time.

"People will open up when they see me, Nikki," he insisted in his know-it-all tone. "I'm adorable. I'm friendly." Did someone have an oversized ego? "Everyone will let down their guard so you can ask your prying questions while I get showered with attention."

He had a point.

Dash plopped his rear end on the seat and sat with his nose in the air like the entitled royalty he thought he was.

End of conversation, so I didn't even attempt to argue. It wasn't worth it. Besides, but I didn't tell Dash dogs weren't allowed in the hospital. Another lesson he would need to learn the hard way.

"How do you plan to get Clive talking?" Audrey asked. "And what are you going to do about Will? I can go in first, scope out the situation, and maybe send some cold breezes through the room or try some eerie noises."

I lifted my muffin bag. "Tasty bribes."

She howled with laughter.

Dash lifted his nose a tad higher and stuck his head forward between the front seats to sniff the bag. "Snacks? You brought snacks? For me?"

"Not for you, Dash." I moved the bag to the floor, away from his drooling snout. "In case your cuteness doesn't work, they're for anyone who needs a little more encouragement to open up."

It couldn't hurt to stroke his ego now and then. Plus, he *was* cute if you liked a somewhat overbearing entitled dachshund.

"I'm still full from breakfast anyways," he said and returned to his statuesque position.

Big surprise there.

I pulled into the Frog Hollow Hospital parking lot. Our town's community hospital–not a Trauma One facility by a long shot, but busy nonetheless. After driving up and down several rows packed with vehicles, I finally spotted an open space at the end of a row in the shade. Bingo. Exactly what I needed for Dash. But before I got there, an old Volvo station wagon slipped in ahead of me.

Without thinking, I laid on my horn, irritated with the driver. But when she parked and slid out of the car, I flushed in embarrassment at my behavior. I should have recognized the car. Fortunately, someone backed out a couple of cars away, and I pulled into that spot, hoping Jane hadn't figured out the annoying honking jerk was me.

I fiddled with the keys and the muffin bag, waiting for Jane to get a head start. But instead of heading toward the hospital entrance, she strutted right to my door and banged on the glass. "What is wrong with you?"

Dash barked furiously. "I need to get out to pee!"

"In a minute." I tried to hush him as I looked sheepishly at Jane.

"Oh, it's *you*," she said as if I amounted to something worse than swamp crud on the bottom of her shoe.

I opened the door, ready to apologize up and down, but Dash lunged past me and jumped up, trying to climb Jane's legs.

"She always has treats, Nikki!"

Jane picked up Dash, gave him a tight cuddle, also kissing the top of his head. "Prince Dasher. I've missed you. You want a treat?" Her tone all sweet and cutesy-pie now.

Dash slobbered all over her face while his tail flew from one side to the other. Of course, his antics improved Jane's mood. She laughed, then put him down so she could fish a treat out of her jean's pocket.

"Nikki, I told you I could help," he said. "She lost her mean voice."

"So," Jane said with her full—and not friendly—attention back on me. "What are you doing here?" Dash took the treat with a dainty nibble without accidentally nipping her fingers.

I spied Audrey hovering behind Jane, thoroughly enjoying my predicament. It was nice to know that my embarrassment was entertaining for someone.

"I'm so glad to bump into you, Jane." I tried to sound as upbeat as possible. "Sorry for honking, but Dash had to get out of the car to..." I cupped my hands around my mouth, "find a bush."

"I did?" he said, looking up at me now instead of showering Jane with more of his adoring puppy dog eyes. "Oh, right. A tree to mark. Thanks for the reminder." He wiggled out of her arms and waddled off just beyond the parking spaces and lifted his leg.

"Has he gained weight since yesterday?" Jane asked. Her scowl indicated this was not acceptable.

I really wanted to say something to the effect that, yes, Dash is a food glutton, and he stole all the breakfast sausages this morning. But I was afraid that might just give her a reason to find a "better" home for him. Instead, I waved her comment off, hoping to put her at ease about my dog parenting skills.

"Dash had a big breakfast, I said. "You know, a little celebration to welcome Honey and Dash into the family. I got a bit carried away. But, don't worry, that was a one-time thing."

Dash returned from taking care of his personal business and sat in front of Jane again. He stared up at her, sending love with his big deep chocolate eyes, and I watched the tension melt completely out of her face. He definitely had a gift when it came to softening up people. At least those that loved dogs. And he knew it.

"Good boy, Dash," I said. Glad for his help.

"Have you heard how Clive is doing?" I asked, bringing the conversation around to what I was actually curious about. I'd assumed that's what brought Jane to the hospital, too.

She glanced at her watch, a big round type with a sweeping second hand that I didn't see too much these days now that everyone used digital. "All I know at this point is that Clive was extremely lucky and should make a complete recovery. In the meantime," she looked over her shoulder, "I'm really shorthanded. Especially since Will never showed up at the shelter this morning. So—"

I cut her off before she made an excuse to leave. "Will is here. There's his motorcycle." I pointed to a barely visible bike, parked haphazardly, not even in an actual spot, but pulled over the curb onto the grass. As far as I knew, it could belong to anyone, but it worked as a distraction.

Jane barely glanced in the direction I'd pointed. "I can't believe it," she said. "He knows I'm short-handed today, and he never answered when I called him. Fortunately, I managed to beg a couple of college kids to come in to clean the kennels, but I could have used Will to supervise. He should have known I'd need him," she mumbled more to herself than to me.

I could imagine Jane's stress level sky-high from the attack, losing her help, and having her shelter under the microscope now.

"Anything I can do?" I'd made that promise to myself to do more for the animals, and heck, it was the perfect opportunity to get inside and do some snooping.

"Oh, you don't know how helpful that would be. Can you walk the dogs? They can't go out unsupervised, and I won't have time."

She made another show of looking at the time, so I knew she was about done with this chat. "As it is, I'm closing the shelter for adoptions until the police are done with their investigation. This whole Clive mess is a terrible disruption."

I put my hand on Jane's arm in a show of solidarity and sympathy. "I'll be over as soon as possible."

"Okay," she answered. "I'm going to check on Clive, and

I'll be back at the shelter in, oh, at least another hour. Don't show up before then."

She stooped and gave Dash another pat on his head. For a moment, I thought she might stand up and do the same to me, but she didn't. I watched as she power-walked toward the hospital in her Nike sneakers, jeans, and a dark blue *Underdog Animal Shelter* t-shirt.

Dash yapped a few times but stayed with me without any encouragement. That must mean progress of some sort.

"Great job keeping Jane out here. It gave me time to check out happenings on the inside," Audrey said as if she was out of breath. Was that even possible for a ghost? I squinted to catch a glimpse of her, but saw only a faint whisper of mist in the passenger seat of my Beemer.

"Did you discover anything?" Fingers crossed because it might save me time snooping around Clive's hospital room.

"You won't believe what I discovered," she said, full of what I could only describe as unbridled excitement. "I can't tell you about it yet, though, because Will is heading straight toward you. If his scowl is any indication, he's not a happy camper. Be careful, Niks," she said, ringing every one of my alarm bells.

And suddenly, I was on my own. Again.

## 24

"Nikki!" Will snapped at my back. I couldn't see him, but his tone made me cringe. "Why did you tell Jane that I was here?" he demanded.

I turned around slowly and pasted a puzzled expression on my face. "Give me a break, Will. Your motorcycle is parked right over there for anyone (I almost said idiot) to see."

Will looked where I pointed and actually let out a sharp laugh. I suppose that was better than yelling, but I didn't know what he found so funny unless he was laughing at himself.

"That?" he said, then shook his head in total disgust. "You thought that scooter was my metallic triton-blue Suzuki GSX sport bike?"

Oops, someone was overly fond of his machine. Motorcycles weren't my forte, and I'd just unknowingly insulted his baby. After a second, more thorough inspection of the offending scooter, my mistake was obvious, even to my untrained eyes. To my credit, though, this one was a similar blue for what that was worth. And, from the way the scooter was pulled between the two cars, it was hard to see all the features without a close inspection.

"Okay, so I'm not a motorcycle aficionado," I said. At best, it was a lame excuse, but I'd jumped to the first conclusion because based on Lacey's information Will was here, but I couldn't divulge that source.

Dash, always eager to say hello (and beg for a treat whether he needed it or not), jumped on Will's legs. Unable to ignore the adorable dachshund, he crouched down to Dash's level. Dash sniffed every bit of Will's shoes while he enjoyed a vigorous back scratch.

Through his ruckus of hearty yips and yaps, I thought I heard Dash say, "His shoes. His shoes. His shoes." I couldn't see what had him so wound up, but the interruption gave me the opening I needed.

"The more important question is, why do you care if Jane knows you're here?" I asked, hoping to get to the heart of the matter.

He took his time to straighten up. Then, he shoved his hands into his pockets and casually leaned against the bumper of my car. Was he practicing his pose for the cover of the latest men's magazine?

"Actually, Nikki, the important question is, why are *you* here?"

I couldn't read his expression, which fell somewhere between cockiness and annoyance. On top of that, I hated it when someone turned the tables on me, so I gave him a dose of his own medicine and changed the subject again.

"I can't help but notice how spiffed up you are this morning, Will."

He smiled like a proud peacock with his tail feathers on full display. Note to self: compliments go right to his head. I filed it away under valuable tactics to remember for future use.

"I didn't think it was appropriate to visit the hospital with all the dog and cat fur covering my clothes." He cocked his head to one side and said, "You clean up pretty well, too."

His eyes traveled slowly from my sandals to my rayon turquoise t-shirt with goldfish swimming diagonally across the front, a favorite gift from Audrey. I crossed my arms over my chest, not enjoying his unwanted scrutiny.

"But," I said now that I had a clear view of his shoes, "your sneakers are badly stained, which totally spoils your overall look. Did you stop to do a little dumpster diving on your way over?"

I laughed and tried to make it sound like a joke because, really, why would I jump to that conclusion if Dash hadn't given me the head's up?

A shadow crossed over his face, barely noticeable if I hadn't been looking for a reaction.

"I've got to get to the shelter," he said abruptly. He started to walk away, but then he stopped and turned around.

"It's strange that you showed up the very day that one person was murdered, another attacked, and you just happened to find Prince Dasher abandoned. Supposedly, all by accident," he added like he didn't believe my story. This quick change of persona threw me off. I didn't like it. What happened to the friendlier version of Will Brooksby?

On impulse, I said, "To answer your earlier question, I'm here to check on Clive and bring him some of Birdie's muffins. Too bad you missed out on them this morning."

I held up the bag. He licked his lips. Should I offer him a muffin? Of course not! He'd lost his opportunity when he skipped Birdie's invitation to breakfast. I continued on my original thread.

"It was awful finding Clive in that pool of blood, and I'd like to know how he's doing and if he saw his attacker. I don't want to be next if that person thinks I know something."

I knew that was a real possibility after finding Vernon and Clive.

Will smacked the side of his head. "I completely forgot about breakfast," he said, sounding genuinely upset. He ran his fingers over the stubble on his chin.

"I keep thinking about every possibility surrounding this murder. To answer your question, I just didn't want to get sidetracked by Jane, okay? My grandfather asked me to visit Clive. He thought I might get him to open up to me since we work together. Didn't happen."

He stared at me without saying anything else, then walked closer. "About the dumpster?" My ears perked up. "Early yesterday, I saw Clive walk to the rear, check if anyone was watching, then he threw a bag into the dumpster. I didn't think too much of it at the time because Clive always acted a bit sketchy. After his attack, though? I went back to see if maybe I could find any clues in that bag."

I knitted my brows. "Why are you telling me this, Will? First, you verbally attack me for being here, and now you're giving me information? I don't get it."

His shoulders slumped. "Yeah, well, I don't get it either. I can't figure you out, but if you can help, I want this solved before anyone else gets hurt. And for the record, I do think you could be in danger. Me too, for that matter."

I glanced in the passenger seat of my car, at Audrey slumped as low as possible, watching us intently.

Could I trust Will, or was he just playing head games?

"So, what are you going to do next?" I asked.

Will dug around in his pocket and pulled out his hand. He opened his palm, revealing a handful of colorful gems, like the ones from Vernon's trunk. I gasped.

He squinted. "You recognize these?" He sounded suspicious.

What could I dare tell him without getting myself into trouble with his grandfather? Heck, I was already in trouble, but I remembered something to help me dodge this bullet.

"I saw gems similar to those on the floor of the kennel where Jane and I found Clive. What do you think it means?"

He let out a long, frustrated sigh. "I wish I knew. Maybe nothing."

I didn't think it was nothing, but I kept that to myself for now.

## 25

After Will walked to his fancy motorcycle and roared away, I picked up Dash, slid onto the cool leather seat of my Beemer, and let out a long sigh of relief.

"That was strange," I said, reviewing the conversation that jumped between an aggressive confrontation and a friendly chat. Which Will Brooksby was the real deal? I wondered. I hoped for the friendly version since it would be a darn shame to waste such handsomeness on a run-of-the-mill jerk.

Possibly, Will was just a confused male trying to sort out his own life. Maybe, maybe not, but at any rate, I didn't have the time to figure out his problems. I had my own.

"Niks, you've got to hear about my visit to Clive's room," Audrey said in a breathless exhale that was more like a breeze through dry leaves than a real voice. I was getting used to the sound and found it comforting in a weird kind of way. Perhaps it helped bring me back to the comings and goings in the hospital parking lot.

"Did you hear something interesting?"

I only half-listened to my grandmother, though she seemed excited to tell me about visiting Clive. But knowing Audrey, it could be that she walked through multiple walls and heard the doctors discussing a gruesome procedure or actually heard Clive telling someone a juicy tidbit. I hoped it was the latter so we could move to the next step. Whatever that was.

"It was more what happened than what I heard," she said. "Although, I guess the two overlap."

I looked at her, focused now. "What are you babbling about?"

"You won't believe this, Niks, but Clive saw me. All five-foot-five of ghost hovering right next to him."

Well, that jerked my attention to high alert.

I twisted around in my seat in one graceful move so as not to disturb Dash until I faced Audrey's shimmery spot.

"What? Is that possible? I mean, yeah, I can see you, and Birdie can, too. But Clive?" That made no sense. "Can't you control that part of your, um, talent? You know, who actually sees you?"

Audrey did her weird shruggy motion that sent a cool breeze over my face. It felt wonderful in the rising morning humidity but also spooky in light of this new information.

"I'm learning new stuff all the time, Niks, and all I can tell you is that I hovered near Clive's bed waiting for someone to come in. I expected Jane or a doctor and assumed they might shed an interesting tidbit of information about Clive."

"And?"

"And... Clive opened his eyes, looked right at me, and said, "Who are you?" If I wasn't a ghost, I might have fainted right there on the spot because I looked around and saw no one else in the room. Just Clive and me staring at each other. Niks, believe it or not, I was in a state of shock."

That was hard to imagine. "So, what did you say to him?"

"I gathered my wits in less time than it takes to scare the socks off a dead guy," she said. "Niks, this is the best part. I said, 'I'm your worst nightmare, Clive.'"

His face went as pale as the sheet covering him. I thought he'd actually died." Audrey laughed and laughed. "I'm really enjoying this more than I should be."

I looked around the parking lot, checking for anyone watching me. People scurried to their car or toward the entrance of the hospital, but no one seemed to pay a lick of attention to me. But just in case, I lifted Dash up to my shoulder to make it look like I was talking to him if someone did happen by and wondered what the heck I was doing sitting in my car talking to myself.

Instead, they'd assume I was talking to my dog, which might be strange to some but totally acceptable as far as I was concerned. Dash rested his head on my shoulder and settled in for a nap. I grabbed the muffin bag with my free hand and helped myself to a snack.

Comfy and ready to hear the rest of Audrey's story, I asked, "Once you got over your shock and scaring Clive to death, did you learn anything helpful?"

"Well, his doctor—very handsome in case you're interested, Niks—walked in and said in a deep voice, 'How are you feeling today?' Clive looked at me again. I gave a little wave to the doctor, but he totally ignored me. The doctor couldn't see me, Niks. Clive looked even more worried, and he said, 'Could the pain meds make me hallucinate?' I added an ooo-ooo to really mess with him."

Now, Audrey's laugh came out more like a series of

snorts, obviously enjoying herself so much I could barely understand her. But, I was pretty sure I got the gist of it despite all the outbursts.

"The doctor asked Clive..." Audrey lowered her voice to mimic his baritone, and even I broke up at her ridiculous imitation. "'Young man, are you hearing voices or seeing people?' Clive answered, 'Both, I think,' in a shaky squeaky voice."

"'Okay,' said the doctor without skipping a beat, and he jotted something in Clive's chart. Then the doctor said, 'You did suffer a nasty concussion along with the shock of the stab wound. I'll lower the dosage and see if that helps.' He scribbled some more, then walked out. Poor Clive was stuck with me. He pulled the sheet over his face, so I left."

I rehashed what Audrey just told me. "So, Clive isn't hallucinating, but he assumes he is. That's handy. We can really mess with him and try to get information. I wonder how long that will last." I nibbled the muffin. Crumbs rained down on Dash. This surprise shower woke him from his nap and sent him into a clean-up frenzy.

"Yummy, Nikki. Thank you. I was getting hungry," he said.

"I wish I knew," Audrey said. "I hope it only lasts as long as it takes to get Clive talking. I feel much safer when I can control who sees and hears me and who doesn't."

Right after Audrey finished her story, I heard Jane's voice. I turned and watched her approach my car. "Why are you just sitting in there?" she asked.

Jeez, she was nosy. Couldn't she tell I was snacking and keeping Dash company? Never mind listening to Audrey's interesting snooping revelations, but that part was for my ears only.

"I decided to wait around for you, Jane. How is Clive doing?" I said like we were best buddies.

She leaned against my car and reached in to ruffle Dash's ear. "To be honest? Clive was as white as a ghost when I got to his room." I resisted the urge to snicker and look in Audrey's direction. "He insisted that he saw someone sitting next to him in his room. He was very agitated about it and told me that the woman even talked to him." I looked at Jane to see if she believed Clive, but she rolled her eyes like he needed serious help.

"Really? Poor guy," I said and shook my head.

"Yeah, I asked the nurse about visitors, but apparently, he only had one visitor before I got there, Will. With this new odd symptom, I'm not sure when he'll be released. Most likely, not today, which leaves me shorthanded at the shelter. Are you positive I count on you to walk a few of the dogs this afternoon?"

I'd make the time. For the dogs. "I already told you I would. I'll try to be there around three."

"Thank you so much," she gushed. "It turns out I can't be there because I have a long list of supplies to pick up, but I'll make sure Will knows you're coming. He'll let you inside and show you which dogs need exercise," she said like she was ticking items off a mental list. "Nikki? I really appreciate this."

Jane's phone rang. She turned away to answer. "Hello?" she said and walked to her car and slipped in so I couldn't eavesdrop.

"Well, you made it onto her short list, Niks. Maybe she finally saw the writing on the wall and knows where her bread is buttered. I'll bet she's missing my generous donations, and she's desperate for you to start sending them again."

I brushed crumbs off Dash's ears. "Oh, that feels good. Don't stop, Nikki," he groaned and happily leaned into my fingers.

I obeyed his request for a few more minutes then said, "Dash? Listen to me. I'm going into the hospital. I won't be gone for long, and you *have* to stay right here in the car. You can't leave. Understand?"

"Yes, Nikki. I can't leave the car unless a squirrel taunts me."

"No! No squirrels or anything else. Stay in the car."

I slipped out. Dash dropped his head between his paws like he was a sulking two-year-old. As far as I was concerned, he had the perfect spot. It was shady with dappled light streaming in through the leaves. The open windows allowed a breeze to keep the car from overheating. He had nothing to complain about. But, in the short time I'd known Dash, I knew he'd think of something. I had to move quickly.

Surprisingly, he said nothing. Just closed his eyes and ignored me. It probably wasn't a good sign.

"Do you think he'll do what you asked?" Audrey whispered. She floated next to me as I walked toward the entrance.

"Maybe you should stay with Dash. Make sure he doesn't get into any trouble."

"Sorry, Niks. Dash is on his own. I'm keeping an eye on you, so *you* don't get into any trouble. Plus, I wouldn't dream of missing out on your chat with my new buddy, Clive." She snorted, a sound like a car backfiring. "That's where you're headed, right?"

"Right. Good timing. I'll ask him about those colored gems I saw in Honey's kennel. Will told me that Clive threw some in the dumpster. Maybe he spilled some and overlooked them. Whatever happened, he's the only connection at this point between the gems Birdie found in Vernon's car, the gems Clive threw in the dumpster, and the ones I saw in Honey's kennel."

"Perfect. Put him on the spot, and if he pretends ignorance, boom! I'll persuade him with my best ghostly talents."

I didn't doubt for a second that Audrey would get Clive talking.

We walked the rest of the way to the entrance in silence.

One important question remained: would Clive provide something... anything, useful?

## 26

Finding Clive's room proved easier than I'd expected. Audrey actually led the way with a faint glimmer here and a cool breeze there. She guided me to the elevator, down the hall, and right into his room, number 402.

Look at us, I thought. Working together like a well-oiled skillet.

I peeked around the open door and saw the first bed neatly made but empty. No roommate. This made everything easier. Clive, in the bed nearest the window, slumped under the covers, propped up against a pile of pillows with the sheet pulled up to his skinny waist, leaving his heavily bandaged left shoulder exposed. A food tray lay untouched on a table next to his bed, and a sad arrangement of half-dead red roses shed their fading petals in a vase on the windowsill. A typical hospital room, by all appearances.

The T.V. blared the news about the Underdog Animal Shelter and Clive's attack. Instead of greeting us, Clive remained glued to the story with his image filling the screen. Was he enjoying this gruesome attention? I had no idea.

I walked in. "Hello, Clive," I said, forcing a smile.

He swung his head around the way it happens when you're completely surprised. His face paled, then he shrank back against the pillows like he hoped they'd swallow him.

"What are *you* doing here again?" he managed to squeak out.

"Again? I haven't been here before, Clive." I walked closer to his bed.

Then it dawned on me; he'd confused me with Audrey. Of course! When she became a ghost, she'd returned as her much younger self. I'd completely forgotten how much we resembled each other—our thick and wavy, light brown hair, same height, weight, and most striking of all, identical intense blue eyes. This was awkward.

He relaxed slightly. "Oh man, I don't know what's real anymore," Clive said and stared at me like he was trying to figure something out.

"I can assure you, Clive, I am a real living, breathing person, not a ghost." I laughed, and he did too, but not very convincingly.

"I just need to ask you a couple of questions, and then I'll get out of your hair. Is that okay?" I sat on the chair near the bed without waiting for an invitation, which might never come.

His eyes narrowed. "You're the babe I saw with Will. You're the one who has that Prince Dasher dog. What do *you* want to know?"

I crossed my legs and dropped my hands onto my lap in the most non-threatening position I could muster. "Clive, I was with Jane when we found you in Honey's kennel. It was very traumatic."

Immediately, I realized how self-centered that sounded. So I added, "For you, of course. I stopped by to find out how you're doing." I blinked several times as if I was holding back tears.

"Oh." His right hand went to the bandage on his left shoulder.

"That looks like quite a wound you got. Did you see who stabbed you?"

He flexed his shoulder and rubbed it. "Naw. I was cleaning the kennel, and whoever it was snuck up behind me. I don't remember anything."

"That's odd," I said.

"It wasn't odd at all. It was horrifying. Imagine if I got shot like Vernon? I might not be here talking to you."

"No. I mean, it's odd that the person attacked you from behind, but your wound is in front." Was I the only one who'd noticed this discrepancy?

Clive puckered his lips like this was the first time he'd considered the oddity. "The guy knocked me down, and I hit my head on the cement floor of the kennel," he said. "I guess I managed to roll onto my back, and then he stabbed me. To be honest, I don't really remember what happened. The doc said I got a concussion."

Was he making this up as he went?

"He?" I asked.

"He. She." He shrugged, throwing both arms out to his side. That caused a grunt, and his face twisted with pain. He gently cradled his left arm and guided it back to lay it across his stomach. "I told you I don't know," he blurted out in anger.

It sure looked like I'd gotten him mighty flustered.

Audrey floated into the room, silently and out of Clive's

view. She stopped right next to his bed. "Clive?" she whispered like a cool breeze.

If I thought I'd startled him when I'd arrived, the shock of Audrey's arrival practically made him levitate off the bed before he covered his eyes with his good arm. I moved and stood opposite Audrey, so he was sandwiched between me, the living, breathing human on one side, and Audrey the ghost, ready to work her skills on the other. Not a good place to be, especially if you had something to hide.

Clive peeked out from under his arm, then his head whipped from me to Audrey. His face went from white to dull gray as he stared at the two of us. Of course, I didn't dare glance at Audrey. Instead, I put a steadying hand on Clive's arm.

"Are you okay? Should I call the nurse?" I asked.

"You don't need a nurse, Clive," Audrey whispered. "You need to unburden your conscience; tell the truth."

Clive looked at me; desperation filled his eyes. "Do you see her, too?"

I made a show of looking around the room, struggling to control my urge to laugh. "I'm not sure who you mean, Clive. It's just you and me in here," I managed to say without a hint of cracking a laugh.

I hooked my foot on the chair behind me, slid it next to the bed, and sat down, eye level with him now.

"Clive," I said. "Look at me and focus."

He turned his head to me, and I almost gagged when I saw his rotten teeth and got a whiff of his putrid-smelling breath wafting from his open mouth. Disgusting! I forced myself not to turn away. At least I had his attention because this might be my one and only chance to grill him.

"Clive. I know you threw colored gems in the dumpster. Why did you do that?"

He huffed, and a stench of rotten egg hit me square in the face. I covered my nose and mouth, faking a cough. This was torture. It had better generate something useful.

"Worthless gems," he said. "It was supposed to be a payoff from Vernon."

I sat up straighter. Maybe we were getting somewhere. "Payoff for what?"

He fidgeted, glanced quickly at Audrey, then back to me. "I shouldn't have said that." Clive clamped his mouth shut, which helped in the stink department, but I wanted information, and I had to get him talking again.

"Vernon is dead. He's not the one who attacked you," I said.

"Tell her, Clive," Audrey said and sent a cold breeze over him as an added incentive.

"Okay. Okay. Maybe it doesn't matter now. I got a call to find a home for the dog, so I connected him with Jane."

"What's so special about the dachshund?" I mean, *I* knew Dash was a super special, even unique dog, but the talking part couldn't be what this was about. No one knew that ability except Audrey, Birdie, and me.

Clive looked at me as if I were a dunce. "The reward?"

Now it was my turn to look confused, which wasn't an act.

"You didn't know?" he said, then laughed like it was the funniest thing he'd ever heard. "Why'd you grab the mutt then?"

Tattoo Guy was getting on my nerves. "I didn't *grab* him, Clive. I found him, abandoned. So I did the humane thing. I picked him up, intending to return him to his owner. It's what people do."

Unless you're a slimebug like Clive, I guess, but I didn't

say that. I wondered where the heck this whole saga was headed.

"The owner's dead."

"I *know* Vernon's dead," I said, but before I could urge Clive to get to the point, he hit me with a doozie.

"No, not Vernon," Clive said impatiently. "The dog's *real* owner. She died and left a fortune. Her relatives didn't want the dog."

He licked his lips like he could taste that fortune. "One of the relatives, a friend of mine, said I'd get a reward if I found a good home for the dog. How crazy is that? Anyway, I convinced Vernon to take the dachshund, and we'd split the reward. It wouldn't look good if I took him 'cause Jane knows I'm not crazy about dogs. I found those gems with the dog's stuff and figured that was the reward, so I split it with Vernon."

"But they turned out to be worthless," I said and sat back, trying to make sense out of this.

"*Those* gems, yeah. Found that out when I showed them to the owner of the jewelry store in town. Just a pile of worthless fancy colored glass, he told me. I wasn't too happy, so I called my friend who put me onto this scheme in the first place. But he insisted I should take another look. Said I'd find something valuable with the dog's belongings."

Clive sat up like he had a spring attached to his back.

"Hey!" he said as if a lightbulb had just flashed in his pea-sized brain. "You have the dog. Do you have his stuff, too?"

Was this guy as dumb as he looked? Did he think we were friends now, and I'd cut him in on the reward if I found it? Fat chance.

"Me? Listen, Clive, when I found the dog, he wasn't sitting in the parking lot with a suitcase or anything.

Wouldn't all his stuff be in Vernon's car? Or, did Vernon double-cross you, so you killed him?"

"What? No! Vernon was okay. He wouldn't do that. He thought those glass gems were worth something when we divvied them up fair and square. It wasn't till later that I found out they were worthless. So, whoever killed Vernon is the person who attacked me. It has to be."

"How many people knew about the reward? Will? Jane? Anyone else?" I asked.

"No idea." He looked around the room and blinked his eyes several times. "Wow. I don't see anyone else in here anymore. Maybe I'm getting back to normal."

Whatever that was.

He reached over to the bedside table, grabbed a piece of gum, and stuffed it in his mouth. That should help his swamp breath.

I saw Audrey hovering near the door like she was ready to get a move on. Apparently, Clive's ability to see her was history, so my secret scary weapon was safe. I wondered what he was planning to do next but not enough to stick around to find out.

I stood up and tucked the bag of muffins under my arm. They were too good for someone like Clive Martin.

"You're leaving?" he whined. Now he wanted company? Go figure.

"I plan to solve this crime before someone else gets hurt." Like me, I thought with a shiver and headed toward the door.

"Wait," Clive said in such a pathetic voice I stopped, turned around, and waited. "Can you feed my cats? Apartment 27A at the Frog Hollow Highlands apartment complex. I asked Jane to bring me clothes, but I forgot to ask her to feed the cats. Tattoo and Pierce."

Really? That's what he'd named his cats?

"Tell Jane to hurry with the clothes if you see her. I can't leave in this thing with no back on it."

I almost laughed at his predicament but just hustled out at a fast walk down the hall. I jabbed the elevator button, then cursed impatiently while I waited. Finally, it dinged. The doors opened. A family poured out, and at last, I stepped inside. Alone. The doors whooshed closed.

"Audrey?" I whispered, "are you here with me?"

Silence.

As soon as the elevator reached the lobby, I hustled to the exit and made a beeline to my car. When I was about fifty feet away, though, I knew something was terribly wrong.

## 27

There was Audrey, zooming around and around the red Beemer like a sheet blowing in a hurricane. She was so agitated, little sparks of light randomly bounced off the car. This was terrible.

My heart pounded out of control as I ran, reaching my car in two seconds flat. I wrenched the car door open and searched every inch inside. Empty. I wanted to scream, but I could barely breathe.

"Dash is gone!" Audrey said, even though I'd already figured that out.

A quick scan of the parking lot turned up nothing. Same with the grassy area. No short-legged dachshund in sight anywhere. I listened for his high-pitched yapping and would even have welcomed his irritating demands at this point. But nothing.

"He wouldn't go far," I said. This, I realized, was a statement I didn't believe.

"What's that under the wiper?" Audrey asked.

I looked. How had I missed that? I pulled out a piece of paper, my fingers shaking uncontrollably as I unfolded it.

Written with a thick black permanent marker, I read: *No dog should be left unattended in a car. I have Prince Dasher. He is safe. Jane*

"Uh oh," I said. "Jane took him."

"She can't do that. It's dognapping. Get in the car, Niks. We have to go to the shelter, and you have to demand him back."

"She's not there. She said she had errands to run." My mind whirled, trying to figure out what to do; where to go. "Clive's house!" I said, happy to have a destination.

"This is no time to get distracted, Niks." Audrey gestured from the passenger seat for me to hurry.

"Jane went to Clive's house." I slid onto the driver's seat. "If I'm fast enough, I'll catch her there."

The car roared to life, and I backed out. Barely looking left or right, miraculously, I managed to screech out of the parking lot without crashing into anything. Thank goodness for luck at this moment of crisis. I took a deep breath and forced my heart rate to slow down and my mind to focus. Somehow, I managed to drive responsibly, arriving at the Frog Hollow Highlands in ten minutes. But was I quick enough to catch Jane?

"We're looking for apartment 27A," I said, turning into the entrance. Fortunately, each apartment had nice big numbers easy for me to read. After one more turn, I spotted Jane's old Volvo in front of the unit on the end of the building.

"There it is, Niks. Pull in behind her, so she can't drive off with Dash."

I pulled right up to her bumper, cutting off any wiggle room to maneuver around me.

"Don't worry," Audrey said. "If Jane tries any funny business, this ghost has your back."

"Funny business? Like what?"

"What if she's the murderer, Niks? Maybe she found that reward Clive babbled about and is worried you're on to her. She took Dash to lure you here, knowing you'd try to get him back. You could be next on her list."

I didn't have that tingly fear feeling running through me, only anger that Jane took Dash. But, I'd be extra careful. "What do you plan to do to help me, Audrey?"

"Good question. I'll think of something, though." And, just like that, she disappeared into thin air, giving me zero reassurance.

I peeked into the Volvo as I scurried by. No Dash. Should I take the front door or follow the path that led around the side of the apartment? Stopping for a moment, I reconnoitered. The end unit meant I had the option of two entrances, front and rear. I chose the path to the rear, hoping for the element of surprise.

As I rounded the corner, the back door of the apartment swung open, and I froze. Jane hustled out with an armful of men's clothes I assumed belonged to Clive.

"Jane?" I said.

"Huh?" She looked my way, tripped, and sent pants, t-shirts, and sneakers flying in every direction. "What are you doing here?" she managed to ask while lying on her side.

"Really? You took my dog," I said and held my hand out to help her up. "Where's Dash?"

She stood, brushed off her pants, and picked up one piece of clothing, then another. Without looking at me, she said, "When I opened the door, Clive's cats ran out. Prince Dasher took off after them. I'm sure he'll come back," she said, then finally looked at me. I didn't see killer in those eyes, only regret with a helping of embarrassment.

"I should have been more careful," she said like it was the most difficult admission she'd ever made.

I couldn't agree more but decided not to rub it in. At this point, I needed to keep her as an ally on my side. "Listen, Jane. Clive needs those clothes. If you take them to him at the hospital, I'll stay here to look for Dash and the cats. Okay?"

Jane put her hand on my arm and squeezed. "I shouldn't have taken him out of your car. He was curled up asleep on the seat, but I panicked, especially after what happened when I let Vernon adopt him. I don't know. I thought you weren't the right person for him. Nikki. I was wrong."

Wow. That's not what I expected to hear, but I'd take it.

"After I find Dash and get the cats inside and fed, I'll go to the shelter like I promised. Don't tell Clive that his cats got out. He has enough to worry about."

Not that I was a fan of Tattoo Guy by any means, but I thought it best to show a little sympathy since he was Jane's relative.

Jane took off her glasses and rubbed her eyes. Stress lines etched a deep map of worry at the edges of her eyes.

"I suppose so, but Clive has a habit of making bad decisions and getting himself in trouble. I've tried to help, but he tends to be his own worst enemy. If he wasn't my nephew..." Jane shook her head and left that thought unsaid, but I could see she'd love to cut him loose. She ended our confrontation by saying, "Anyway, I'll get going now."

I had to move my car to allow Jane to leave. I backed onto the street and parked in front of the next apartment, out of anyone's way. As soon as Jane drove off, I sensed Audrey next to me.

"Okay, so I was wrong about Jane. But you never know,

Niks. She's in a no-win situation with that rotten nephew. What's your plan to find Dash?"

"Food!" I said then grabbed the muffin bag. In a flash, I returned to the back of the apartment, shook the bag, and scattered muffin chunks on the ground. I hoped Birdie never discovered I'd used her muffins for dog bait, but it seemed like the best chance to lure Dash back to me. If I'd learned anything about that dachshund, he couldn't resist a treat. If this didn't work, then I'd panic.

As I made a trail with the muffin bits, I also scanned along the edges of the adjoining apartments, under bushes, and even under cars. The apartment complex had plenty of hiding places for cats and a short-legged dachshund, but I was confident that food would work.

I ran into Clive's apartment and grabbed a bag of cat food lying next to the fridge. A knife on a magnet strip made quick work of opening the bag, and I was outside again.

"I found the cats!" Audrey said. "They're under that old Subaru. They look like they're scared to death, so don't rush over or they might take off again."

I approached slowly. The car, tireless and perched on cement blocks, made for an excellent hiding spot. "Kitty, kitty, kitty," I called in a soft voice. "Come on, Tattoo. Come on, Pierce." I shook the cat food bag around the car and sprinkled more on the ground.

"What ridiculous names!"

I whirled around and saw Dash trotting along the cement walkway toward me.

"I mean, who picked out those names?" he said. I chuckled because it was a case of the pot calling the cats, well, you know what I mean. His name was over the top even though it suited him to a T.

"Does Birdie know you spilled her muffins on the ground? Delicious, too," he mumbled, licking his chops.

"No, and you aren't going to tell her, Dash. Where the heck did you run off to? I've been worried sick."

Now that I knew he was safe, irritation replaced my anxiety.

"Wow! Stop right there, Nikki. I hid until Jane left so she couldn't take me back to one of those cages. Did you know she dognapped me right out of your car? I was right in the middle of a dream, too. A good one. I can't remember what it was about, but food was definitely part of it. Sausages, I think. Will Birdie cook up more sausages for me?"

I scooped him up and hugged him tight. He struggled a little but not like he really wanted to get away. This little guy had wormed his way into my heart, and I was pretty sure he knew it.

"Hey, pay attention," Audrey said. "The cats are following the food trail back inside. Don't let them get away."

"Cats!" Dash yelped. "Get those cats!"

Reluctantly, I put him down so I could focus on the cats, but Dash had other plans. He charged and herded them inside before I could even blink.

"Close the door, Nikki!"

I did and decided to do a bit of snooping since I was here.

Who wouldn't, right?

## 28

Clive's apartment was shockingly tidy. The counters in the kitchen were spotless, the sink empty of dirty dishes, and the floor spic and span. I peeked into the living room, which was equally organized. One of the cats was already curled up on a blue blanket draped over the sofa. I suppose I shouldn't have been surprised since Clive did an excellent job cleaning the kennels. I reminded myself not to judge someone based on their appearance. That being said, Clive was hiding something. I was sure of that.

"I'm thirsty, Nikki. I need a drink!"

Dash's demand didn't irritate me too much after his disappearance, but he definitely needed a gentle reminder. "Please?" I said.

"Please," he said politely. Was that progress?

I found a bowl and gave him water, plus I cleaned and filled the cat's bowls with water and canned food.

"Heads up, Niks," Audrey whispered. "A car just dropped Clive off. He's walking to the front door."

I glanced out the front window. Sure enough, Clive,

dressed in nurses' scrubs, hurried up the walkway. That made less sense than Dash ignoring a sausage dropped on the floor. "He should still be at the hospital," I said.

A cold tingling ran up my spine. I knew as sure as my eyes were blue that I didn't want him to find me in his apartment. I tucked Dash under my arm and quietly let myself out the back door. He leaped down as I picked up the muffin bag, ready to hightail it to my car, but Dash had another plan.

He ran back to the door, scratching like he was desperate to get inside. "The cats, Nikki!" he said. "You have to talk to those cats."

"The cats are fine, Dash. They have food and water. You do know that I can't actually have a conversation with them like I talk to you, right?"

"But I smelled them there."

"Where?"

"That blanket over the body. I keep telling you. The cats were there," Dash insisted.

That got my attention. I should have paid attention sooner. Not that I thought the cats were there, but the cat-scented blanket was. Unfortunately, the delay and commotion gave Clive time to fling the door open to find us on his back step. His eyes narrowed.

"Muffin?" I held the bag up in a last-ditch effort to throw him off his game.

It did, but only momentarily. Then, a smile slowly spread across his face. Nothing friendly. Nope, it was a cold, calculating grin foretelling something sinister.

I smiled and took a step toward him. Surprised at my bold move, he stepped back, giving me the upper hand. I studied Clive's face, a twitch at the edge of one eye, clamped jaw, and flared nostrils. Items from the last twenty-four hours that had been swirling through my brain—blue blanket, gum, knife, stab wound, cats—flashed again. Now, they fell into place and gave me the ammunition I needed to get to the bottom of this mystery.

"Where's the reward, Clive?" I asked in a calm, I-know-what-you're-up-to tone.

"That's exactly what I want to talk to you about," he said, but his voice sounded shaky and uncertain. "You found Vernon, so you tell me." He sneered like he was so smart. "Clever, right? Asking you to come feed my cats."

He laughed. Again, though, a shaky uncertainty contradicted his cocky attitude.

No, Clive wasn't clever at all. He had no idea that he'd just revealed such an important detail. There was only one way he could possibly know I'd found Vernon's body.

"The cats, Nikki. I told you there were cats where we found the body," Dash kept repeating. Of course, Clive only heard crazy yapping.

"That's the mutt that everyone's all nutty about?"

I picked up Dash and stroked him, muttering, "It's okay."

I saw Audrey hovering in the background. I also saw the blue-handled knife I'd used to open the cat food. I'd carelessly dropped it on a stool next to the door when I'd run out with the bag. I took another step toward Clive. I was close enough now to reach the knife. Again, he stepped backward.

"There's something you should know, Clive," I said.

"That's not how this works. I do the talking." He tried to sound tough, but I suspected my confidence and lack of fear threw him off. If I was correct, Clive only had one plan—scare and intimidate, which wasn't working.

"I'll tell you anyway. Your ghost friend is behind you." I grabbed the knife and pointed it toward Clive.

I saw Audrey grin. She'd been watching and waiting patiently for the perfect moment to work her ghostly charm for the greatest impact. She wrapped her cold, misty arms around Clive. He shivered. He stiffened. Fear consumed him as if he knew something was very wrong. Then, he looked around and even slashed through the air with his arms, but Audrey continued to sway, sending waves of cold air over him.

"What is happening?" he yelled. His sneery macho image now just a puddle of piddle at his feet.

"I warned you, Clive. You know what you have to do," I said and waved the blue-handled knife.

That's all it took for him to reach for his wounded shoulder and slump to the floor. He skootched back until his back was against the cupboard, muttering nonsense the whole time.

Did we go overboard? No. He deserved every bit of terror that overwhelmed him.

"Can I bite him, Nikki? Please? He deserves it."

"Sit, Dash. No biting unless he moves."

Clive's eyes widened even more than I thought was possible.

"Okay, Clive. Why did you kill Vernon?"

"I didn't!"

I waved the knife close to his face. "Are you sure?"

"Okay. Okay. He said he'd found the real reward, and I could forget about getting a single penny of it. I couldn't let him get away with treating me like a piece of worthless garbage."

I nodded, satisfied that he was telling the truth, as horrible as it was. "And then you stabbed yourself to throw suspicion on Jane or Will?"

He nodded. "And you. I saw you when you found

Vernon. You had the dog, and I figured you had his stuff, too. I figured you had the real valuables." He slipped a piece of gum from his pocket and popped it in his mouth.

"You figured wrong about all that, Clive. I have no idea what or where any valuables are. As far as I'm concerned, Dash is reward enough for me." I gave Dash a squeeze, and he licked my chin. He was being surprisingly quiet at the moment.

The front door opened. "Nikki?"

"More company," I said. "In the kitchen, Will."

"Jane asked me to help you find the cats and..." Will stopped dead in his tracks and stared at me, brandishing a knife while Clive cowered on the floor.

"You'd better call your grandfather, Will. Clive here has a long story to tell him. Right, Clive?" I tilted my head and raised my eyebrows to make sure he knew I was serious.

Clive nodded. What choice did he have? I stood over him with the knife. Dash growled, and Audrey continued sending her cold breeze his way. Even if he couldn't see her anymore, his experience in the hospital let him know that he couldn't count out that a ghost had his number.

While we waited, I told Will what I'd learned. He couldn't believe it.

Once the police arrived, I gave my statement, and Officer Brooksby let me leave with Dash. Audrey left too, but of course, Clive was the only one that might figure that out.

But who would believe that part of his story?

Audrey and I enjoyed a well-deserved laugh on the ride back to Moonlight Mansion. With the top down, I savored the canopy of twinkling stars above us. Dash howled while the wind whipped his ears every which way. It sounded like he was singing about sausages, but I couldn't be sure.

Life was grand.

## 29

I thought I'd finally get to sleep in on Wednesday morning, but Dash had other ideas. Of course.

"Wake up, Nikki! Wake up! Nice guy just drove in. I heard his noisy two-wheel driving thing."

I opened my eyes. Honey jumped off the bed and joined Dash at the French doors overlooking the garden below. Why was Will here?

"Lacey drove in, too. Everyone I love. Open the door! I smell sausage!"

"Did you forget something, Dash?"

He looked at me. "Please? Please, Nikki! I love you, too!"

I chuckled. I still couldn't believe this adorable, complicated, demanding dachshund had chosen me as the one person he could talk to. I wasn't sure I'd ever get used to this aspect of our relationship, but I was all in on the journey.

I opened the door, and the two dogs tore down the stairs.

When I turned around, Audrey said, "You did great, Niks." She stood by the balcony's French doors where the dogs had been watching the world below.

"*We* did great, Audrey. We're in this together, remember? You and me."

She let out a long slow sigh. "It's not the same for me, though. But that's okay. You proved to everyone and more importantly to yourself that Nikki Knight is a force to be taken seriously. I'm really proud of you, Niks."

I choked up a little and desperately wished I could hug Audrey. As soon as I had the thought, I felt her arms around me, just like she used to embrace me when I needed that extra bit of love. I don't know exactly what just happened, but I supposed there was still plenty to learn about how we communicated with each other.

"Before you go downstairs, Niks, I have something to show you."

I watched as Audrey floated to the small antique corner desk where she used to sit to write letters. "Come closer, Niks. You can't see it from across the room."

I walked over and stood next to her. A book lay on the desk, but unlike any I'd ever seen before. The title—The Accidental Ghost—shimmered with a faint yellowish glow and appeared to hover above the actual cover. I should have questioned my eyesight, but with all the strange happenings lately, this fit into my new normal.

"Open it," Audrey said.

As my fingers slowly reached out, the cover opened by itself. One piece of paper lay inside with one sentence typed on it in bold gold letters.

*Use your special powers wisely.*

"What special powers?" I asked.

"That's the thing, Niks. You have special powers you don't even think about.

I looked at her, confused.

"Intelligence, curiosity, being true to yourself, and especially, you always stand up for what you believe in. Everything that makes you Nikki Knight are your special powers.

I picked up the paper and flipped it over. Blank. "This is all there is in this book?"

Audrey shrugged. "It's all there is right now, but if you want my opinion, I think more will appear when the time is right. And one more thing," she said. There always seemed to be one more thing with Audrey. I waited.

"Birdie searched every item that she took from Vernon's trunk."

"And? Did she find a treasure hidden somewhere?"

"She found an interesting piece of paper stuck in Dash's vet folder. I didn't understand the legal gibberish, but Birdie explained that whoever has possession of the paper is Dash's rightful guardian. So, guard it carefully, Niks."

"That's a no-brainer," I said. "Dash and I are linked forever as far as I'm concerned. He made that quite clear. No treasure then?" Not that it mattered.

"Nope. Vernon must have been lying to Clive about that."

"So, he got murdered for nothing," I said. "What a waste."

"It is what it is, Niks. Now, my dear, you need to get yourself downstairs. Guests have arrived, and you are the hostess of this mansion.

How could I forget that?

I brushed and braided my hair, pulled on my silkiest, soft moonlight blue t-shirt that perfectly matched my eyes, and a pair of white capris. With a feeling of intense pride, I raced down the stairs, enjoying the coolness of each wooden tread under my bare feet.

"Nikki! Look at the feast Birdie made!" Dash said when I

entered the dining room. "She made my special recipe of beef, rice, and carrots. Will you add sausage pieces? Please?"

How could I resist?

"Good morning, everyone," I said, then added the sausage to Dash's bowl before I sat at the head of the table. On one side, Lacey's voice bubbled with her oversized portion of charm as she talked to Will. Flirted might be the more appropriate term. He sat quietly next to her, and from what I could gather, it looked like he was only half-listening. I focused my attention on Birdie.

Birdie waved her hand around the table. "Just a small celebration for you, Nikki."

"This is amazing, Birdie. Thank you," I said, ready to dig in.

"I didn't have a chance to properly spoil you when you arrived so... better late than never. I made all your favorites: veggie and cheese omelet. Popovers, hash browns, peach shortcake, and mocha hot chocolate with whipped cream and a sprinkle of cocoa powder. Did I forget anything, Nikki?"

"Forget anything? I laughed. "This feast will last the whole week."

She eyed Will's plate. "Not with the way that one is eating. He's making up for missing my spread yesterday." She gave him her raised eyebrow that probably meant, don't let that happen again. "Will dropped in with that beautiful, I'm-sorry centerpiece, so I asked him to stay."

The flowers—pink and white peonies, with sprigs of ivy —scented the room with their amazing fragrance.

Will blushed.

Lacey slid peach shortcake onto her plate. "What's your next case, Nikki?"

Will jerked his head in my direction, and he stared at me. My face burned.

"Next case?" he asked in a tone that really meant what kind of nonsense is this? Or, so I imagined.

"Yeah, Nikki's doing detective stuff. You didn't know?" Lacey said as she dumped a big dollop of whipped cream on top of the shortcake.

"No, I didn't know, but it sounds very interesting."

What was that supposed to mean? I waved away this conversation as if it was all just silly talk.

"Lacey exaggerates," I said. "Of course, I'm interested in what's happening in Frog Hollow now that this is my *forever* home." I stressed the forever for Will's benefit in case he had any designs on getting Moonlight Mansion away from me. "So, if that means I ask questions and make some people uncomfortable, so be it."

I helped myself to a big bite of Birdie's omelet to signal I was done with this part of the conversation. As far as I was concerned, with Honey on one side, Dash on the other, and Audrey somewhere watching my back, if people didn't like me digging into mysteries, that was their problem.

I didn't have to explain myself to anyone.

What surprise would be next?

I had no idea. For now, I planned to enjoy my new home, and all that was dear to me.

### *The End*

**Thank you for reading the Accidental Ghost Detective Series!**

**Sign up for my newsletter and never miss a new release.**

# ABOUT THE AUTHOR

Emmie Lyn grew up in a small town in New England, much like the towns where her female characters live—scenic, quaint and filled with colorful characters. She loves to create mysteries with twists and unexpected turns that draw readers in and capture their imagination.

Emmie lives in rural Massachusetts with her husband, a sweet rescue terrier, and a black cat with a bad attitude. She shares twelve acres with a wide variety of wildlife including deer, bunnies, turkeys, and many songbirds. When she's not busy thinking of ways to kill off a character (for a book, of course!) she enjoys a cup of tea and chocolate in her flower garden, hiking, or spending time near the ocean.

# MORE BY EMMIE!

More books by Emmie Lyn

**Little Dog Diner Cozy Mystery Series**
- Mixing Up Murder
- Serving Up Suspects
- Dishing Up Deceit
- Cooking Up Chaos
- Crumbling Up Crooks
- Dicing Up Disaster

**Mint Chocolate Chip Mysteries**
- Claws of Justice
- Ginger Danger
- Tabby Trouble
- Tuxedo Bravado
- Furgone Conclusion
- Calico Conflict

**Dogs and Donuts Cozy Mystery Series**
- Sprinkles and a Situation

Icing and an Incident
Custard and a Crisis

## Gold Coast Retriever Series
Helping Hanna
Shielding Shelly

## MORE BOOKS LIKE THIS

Welcome to Whiskered Mysteries, where each and every one of our charming cozies comes with a furry sidekick... or several! Around here, you'll find we're all about crafting the ultimate reading experience. Whether that means laugh-out-loud antics, jaw-dropping magical exploits, or whimsical journeys through small seaside towns, you decide. So go on and settle into your favorite comfy chair and grab one of our pawsome cozy mysteries to kick off your next great reading adventure!

*Visit our website to browse our books and meet our authors, to jump into our discussion group, or to join our newsletter. See you there!*

**www.WhiskeredMysteries.com**

## WHISKMYS (WĬSK'MƏS)

**DEFINITION:** a state of fiction-induced euphoria that commonly occurs in those who read books published by the small press, Whiskered Mysteries.

**USAGE:** Every day is Whiskmys when you have great books to read!

LEARN MORE AT https://whiskeredmysteries.com

Made in United States
Orlando, FL
02 February 2023

29376072R10125